melville house classics

STEMPENYU

STEMPENYU

SHOLEM ALEICHEM

TRANSLATED BY HANNAH BERMAN

MELVILLE HOUSE PUBLISHING
HOBOKEN, NEW JERSEY

FIRST PUBLISHED IN 1888 IN *FOLKSBIBLIOTEK*; FIRST
PUBLICATION IN ENGLISH WAS BY METHUEN & CO. (LONDON,
1913).

SERIES DESIGN: DAVID KONOPKA

MELVILLE HOUSE PUBLISHING
300 OBSERVER HIGHWAY
THIRD FLOOR
HOBOKEN, NJ 07030

WWW.MHPBOOKS.COM

FIRST MELVILLE HOUSE PRINTING: DECEMBER 2007
ISBN 13: 978-1-933633-16-9
PRINTED IN CANADA

A CATALOG RECORD FOR THIS BOOK IS
AVAILABLE FROM THE LIBRARY OF CONGRESS

TO MY DEARLY BELOVED GRANDFATHER
REB MENDALLE MOCHER SEPHORIM

To my dear grandfather, greetings!

Stempenyu, my first long novel, which I inscribe to you, is yours; not only because I have the honour to inscribe it to you, but also because it was you who instilled into me the desire to write such a novel. In one of your letters you said to me:

"I should have advised you not to write a novel. Your tastes, and your genre, lie elsewhere. And I doubt if there is anything as romantic in the lives of our people. They are so different from the rest of the world that one must understand them perfectly, before attempting to write about them!"

Your words sank deep into my heart; and I began to realize how much, and in what way, a Jewish novel must differ from all the other novels. The truth is that the circumstances under which the Jew falls in love, and declares his passion, are altogether different from the circumstances which control the lives of other men. Besides, the Jewish nation has its own peculiarities—its own habits, and manners, and customs. And, our national symbols have remained unchanged in spite of everything. And, these too, must have their place in the Jewish novel if it is to bear a true resemblance to Jewish life.

All this came home to me very forcibly after hearing you talk. And, the desire sprang up within me to incarnate what I learnt from you in the persons of the novel—Rochalle the Beautiful, who plays the leading role, and all the others who take their several places in the novel, revolving around the life of Rochalle as the moths fly around a candle.

How much stress I have attained is a different question. My aim was to write a novel in strict accordance with your wishes; that is, according to the views you have expressed regarding the requirements, and the equipment of every Jewish novelist.

And, in this also is *Stempenyu* yours, dear grandfather—the name is yours, and the ideas in it are yours. I found amongst your later works a reference to the connection between Stempenyu and a love-philtre. That was enough to recall to my mind all the wonderful stories I had heard at school about Stempenyu. My imagination was fired. Memory aided me, and the story of the following pages came into being.

It may be that in my district, in Lithuania, the Jews have never heard anything of Stempenyu. And, for that reason, the name may sound rather strange to them—perhaps a little wild. But, for that again, the name is well known in every town and village lying between

Tasapevka and Yehupetz, to say nothing of the towns and villages of your neighborhood—Gennillophatzka, Tsviattsetss, and Tunneyadevka. The youngest child in any of these places knows who Stempenyu was, whom he sprang from, and after what fashion his proud life was spent.

But, I did not intend to centre all the interest exclusively in Stempenyu. I meant to distribute it among three persons, or as they might be called, three characters: the Jewish artiste, Stempenyu, and his fiddle; the Jewish girl, Rochalle, in all her Jewish purity, nobility of thought and action; and, the Jewish woman, Freidel, whose talent for business led her into an exaggerated anxiety about money. These were figures which stood up before me, each in a world of his or her own. And, these three, Stempenyu, Rochalle, and Freidel, are seated on a daïs at the top of the tent, so to speak, while all the rest of the figures in the novel sit over against them, or move here and there, backwards and forwards, in full view of the three principal characters, and flit in and out under their eyes. It was for this reason—because they only pass up and down before the three, and do not take any perceptible part in the story—that I have sketched their characters and doings in the fewest words possible.

I imagine that our Jewish musicians, our composers and our players, live in a manner peculiar to themselves alone. And, it is worth while investigating their mode of living with far more care and insight than I can lay claim to having brought to bear on the musicians portrayed in this novel. To do justice to the task, one must possess, dear grandfather, your penetration, your powers of description, and your experience. Where is one to get these qualifications? How can one hope to gain your courage and your patience?

"Over any work," you wrote me in another letter, "over any piece of work, dear grand-child, one must sweat and toil. One must work, and work at chiseling every separate word to perfection. Remember what I say to you—one must keep on chiselling, and chiselling."

Chiselling! In this lies the whole secret of the woes of all us who are still young. We have never the time to chisel. We rush off to get the whole of our plans completed while standing on one foot, as the saying goes. We wish to finish as well as to begin everything in the one breath. We cannot stop to think out each argument we employ; and, certainly, not to chisel each and every separate word. We have not the patience for these slow growths.

I know, dear grandfather—I feel how necessary it would be to purify Stempenyu through many waters. In your hands, the book would have taken on an altogether different appearance. It would have been a different book from what it is. You would have made of it a story about a story, a story within a story, and a story in itself as well.

"I should like," you wrote in another letter, "I should like that in a book there should be not only beauty of form, but also truth, and depth, and sympathy, as we find in life itself. There should be something to think about as well as to amuse!"

But, the secret of how to bring in these qualities remains with you. No one else has been able to discover it. Only you can create pictures that have many sides to them—a right side and a left, an outer covering and a lining, so to say. Only you can make the Yiddish novel something which is at once clear and mystical. Therefore, it comes about that you are the only true artist in our literature. So that we young folks dare not liken ourselves to you. We are profoundly thankful if we manage to write a plain story without deformities, having all its limbs and members, according to the simplest laws and canons of literature.

Beloved grandfather, will you accept this little offering from me—my first Yiddish novel? I can only accept the hope that it will give you some measure of happiness to know that you inspired it. Perhaps it will appeal to you because I took its name from one of your works. I dare scarcely hope that you will find in its pages something which will meet with your approbation. That I may provide you with a few hours' amusement is the most that I can hope for.

Wishing you all the good in life hat you can possibly wish for yourself, I remain, your devoted grandchild,

THE AUTHOR
KIEFF, 1886

STEMPENYU

STEMPENYU was the nickname he inherited from his father. His father—peace be unto him—was called Berrel Bass, or Berrel Stempenyu, after the village of Stempenyu in the district of Tasapevka. Berrel played the double-bass, was a good story-teller, and a wit, and could invent pretty rhymes. He suffered from an incurable disease, and played at weddings in the disguise of a beggar. He could also amuse the company by turning up his eyes, making grimaces, dancing like a bear, and imitating all sorts of sounds. He had a weakness for playing practical jokes, such as throwing water on the floor in the middle of the dancing, and pinning to the backs of the wedding guests anything he could lay his hands on.

The talent for music was inherited in their family for many generations. Stempenyu's father, Berrel Bass, played the double-bass, as his nickname indicated.

Berrel's father, Shmulik, played the trumpet; and his father, Phillip, played on the harpsichord; and Phillip's father was Ephraim Fiddler, because of his talent for playing the fiddle. In short, Stempenyu was descended from innumerable generations of musicians. Nor was he ashamed of the fact that they all had lived by their playing. He was not at all like the average Jewish workman who thinks it is fashionable to be ashamed of the work in his hands. And, it was true also that Stempenyu had nothing to be ashamed of. It was no trifling matter to make the name he had made for himself in the district of Tasapevka—in the whole world, almost. It was no laughing matter for a man to bear the name of Stempenyu.

Amongst the things which people of the district found to make a boast of was that they had heard Belser the Chasan sing, Gadig the jester preach or lecture, and Stempenyu play. From that you can gather that Stempenyu was not an ordinary, everyday musician—a mere nobody. He was the musician of his day. And, it stands to reason that he could not have become so famous amongst the great ones of the district unless he had in him something exceptional—something which lifted him high above the other players. From time immemorial, we Jews have loved music, and have understood what it really is. Even our worst enemies could not deny this. But, on the other hand, few of us have had an opportunity to hear good music. What are we, that we should seek to amuse ourselves, and to pass the time pleasantly in singing and dancing? Surely our lives are not empty or free from care? We have enough anxieties to keep us from thinking of what is pleasant or enjoyable. But, say what you will, we are excellent judges of good music—of singing as well as playing. Whenever a Cantor makes his appearance in our midst, we rush off to buy to tickets to hear him, let them cost us a meal, even. And, when a good musician plays at a wedding-feast, we are delighted. Whilst, to hear an orchestra playing any piece, by preference a sad one, we feel that it would be well worth walking all day and all night to reach the village to hear it. There is nothing in the world to compare with such a pleasure. And, when it does come to us once in a while, we do not fail to appreciate it. No sooner has the orchestra struck the first note than a profound silence falls upon us all. We sit still and listen; and, the music is always sad, pathetic, melancholy, or at least, in a minor key. The fiddle starts weeping, and loses itself in mournful cadences. And, the other instruments join in, sighing, weeping, sobbing aloud, as one might say. A feeling as of depression comes over us all. It is very nice, the music; but, it makes a man feel depressed. Somehow, every single one of us is plunged into the profoundest melancholy. We cast down our heads, and, our fingers occupy themselves with the table-cloth, or we busy ourselves in making little pyramids from the crumbs of bread which are on the table before us. Our thoughts are deep, and our reflections are bitter; for, each one of us is reminded of his or her personal troubles. Who does not know that no individual in our nation need go about laughing for want of something to feel sad about?

And, it always comes about that we combine the pathos of the music with the pathetic notes that come into our lives every hour of the day. Every separate tone is echoed and re-echoed in our souls. The fiddle especially seems to resound within us again, and yet again.

The heart itself is like a fiddle; the Jewish heart, I mean, of course. The tightly drawn strings want but the lightest touch, and they send forth a variety of sounds—deeply pathetic, wailing, weeping sounds.

A man of talent—a Stempenyu—wrings the very souls out of the Jews.

Oh, what a man Stempenyu was! His talent was without beginning and without end. He would snatch up the fiddle, and drawing the bow across it in the most careless fashion, he would succeed in making it speak at once. It needed but a single movement of his elbow, and the little fiddle was speaking to us all. And, how it spoke! In the most unmistakable accents! Really, with words that we all understood, in the plainest fashion, as if it had a tongue, and as if it were a real living, human being! It would moan, and wail, and weep over its sad fortune, as if it were a Jew. And, its cry was shrill and heartrending. It was as if every note found its way upwards from out the deepest depths of the soul.

Stempenyu would throw his head to one side, whilst his long sweeping locks fell wildly about his shoulders and the nape of this neck. And, his black eyes were wide open, staring vacantly out in front of him, seeing nothing for all the fire that burned in them. His face became deathly pale. It took but a few seconds for Stempenyu to become a different man. He was not the same Stempenyu. He was the incarnation of music itself. One could only see in him a hand that flew up and down, up and down. One heard all sorts of sounds; and, every melody in existence was poured forth from the fiddle like a living stream—a fountain. And, always, everything was lonely and sad—so sad that one's heart was sure to contract within one's body with inexpressible emotion. One's very soul was drawn out of one's body, and, weakness, faintness, almost overcame one—exhaustion.

The people began to feel as if they were dying, dying, going out with a flicker—and, no more.

That is how the Jews felt when Stempenyu was playing his little fiddle for them. They were rendered powerless to do anything but sigh, and weep, and moan.

And, Stempenyu—what of him? He did not seem to be in the least conscious of where he was, and what he was doing. He did not seem to have the faintest notion of the tortures which his playing brought upon the highly wrought nerves of his audience. He simply went on playing and playing, drawing out the deep, deep notes that are at once so beautiful and so terrible to listen to. That is all.

Invariably, it was his habit to finish up his playing by drawing the bow across the strings, from beginning to end, as if he would bind into one note, one last effort, the whole of what he had already played. This done, he folded his little fiddle into his heart, and sat down. His eyes were burning like the starts on a frosty night; and, his countenance shone as with a heavenly light.

The people awoke out of their reveries with a sigh—out of their sad but sweet reveries. And, all at once, the room was filled with noise and hubbub. The tension was broken; and, in half a hundred different voices, there arose a chorus of praise and wonderment. Nobody could find the words enough to express his keen delight and his enthusiasm. And, out of the din, one heard the name of Stempenyu repeated again, and yet again.

And the women? Of them there is nothing at all to

say, except that it is doubtful if they ever shed so many tears in their lives. It may be that they wept as freely over a personal bereavement, on the Day of Atonement, as they did on hearing Stempenyu play his mournful songs. Even the most pious Jew need not shed so many tears over the destruction of Jerusalem as the women were in the habit of shedding when Stempenyu was playing.

The women generally expressed their praises of the music after a different fashion from that employed by the men. They always found some personal wish through which to express their emotions—some wish which showed that their desires were awakened, their inner feelings brought into play.

"I hope that God will help me to able to engage Stempenyu to play at the wedding-feast of my youngest daughter. That is all I wish for now!"

And, as for the young girls—the mademoiselles! They stood stock still, as if they were rooted to the spot. They could do nothing else but stare with wide-open eyes and mouth at the wonderful Stempenyu and his fiddle. They felt that they must not on any account attempt to move a limb, or even blind an eyelid. There was a dead silence amongst them. Only here and there a little heart beat wildly, romantically—tick, tick, and tick! And, here and there a little sigh, so soft and low as scarcely to be heard, managed to make its escape from a little heaving breast.

The tumult and the excitement that arose when Stempenyu and his orchestra made their appearance in a village, and the enthusiasm which prevailed the whole time that he stayed there, are quite beyond description.

"Look! I can see a huge covered wagon drawn by several horses making its way towards us. Can that be the wedding guests—the bridegroom and his people?"

"Not at all. That must be the musicians—Stempenyu and his orchestra."

"Oh, Stempenyu! Do you think that Stempenyu has come already? And, won't it be a fine, jolly wedding, that of Chayam-Benzion Glock's daughter—won't it?"

The news of Stempenyu's arrival coming spread like wildfire. Every single inhabitant of the village felt as if Stempenyu was going to pay him or her a special visit. The women blushed scarlet, and the young girls rushed off to braid and plait their long hair; while the little boys tucked up the legs of their trousers, to avoid the mud splashing on them, and rushed forward with leaps and bounds to meet Stempenyu's wagon as it slowly came into the village. And, even the old men with the long beards and the big families, did not stop to hide their joy at the news that Stempenyu was coming to play at the wedding that was about to take place in their midst. They forgot their dignity; they even forgot their duty and responsibility towards the younger generation. Their dignity and decorum they cast into winds. They were too overjoyed to consider these matters of which they seldom lost sight on any occasion. But, after all, this was something altogether exceptional. Why should they not rejoice? Why should they remember anything when they were not going to pay the costs of bringing over Stempenyu and his orchestra to play at the wedding?

By the time the covered wagon arrived at the door of the inn, the street which constituted the village proper was thronged with people, all of them burning with curiosity to catch sight of the famous Stempenyu and his famous orchestra, as they descended from the wagon to enter the inn. The people were so close to the wagon that there was hardly room for its occupants to alight.

"See here how they are pushing!" they cried one to the other. At the same time they increased their efforts to push still closer to the wagon. As is the habit of Jews, each one wanted to be in the very front of the crowd.

"See here how they are driving their elbows to get before everyone. What is there to see—I should like to know? They are only musicians, the same as other musicians!"

Complaints filled the air, but no one showed the least slackness of effort. The whole villageful of people wanted to stand beside the wagon.

Presently the musicians began to descend, one by one.

First of all came Yekel Double-bass, who was called after the instrument he played. He was a cross-looking Jew with a flat nose, and cotton-wool in his ears. After him came Reb Leibess with his clarionett—a sleepy-looking Jew with thick lips. Next came Chaikel the flute-player—the well-known Chaikel, carrying his flute. Later there descended from the wagon a black, burly Jew whose whiskers grew almost into his eyes, so that he looked like a wild man from the desert. He had such thick eyebrows that it filled one with fear to look at him. That was Reb-Shnayer-Mayer, the accompanist, the second fiddle, that is. Then there jumped out from the wagon several young men, ugly and wild-looking, with downcast eyes, swollen cheeks, and large protruding teeth which resembled small flat shovels. They were only apprentices, who were at present working for Stempenyu for nothing, but who were hopeful that in the course of time they would become famous musicians. And, at the very last, there crept out of the wagon, on little crooked legs, the yellow Michsa the drummer, pulling after him a drum that was much bigger than he was himself. Mischa was just beginning to grow a beard—a little yellow beard that covered only one side of his face, the right side, leaving the left side as smooth as was his forehead. You must know that this same Michsa was married when he was already thirty years old. He took to wife a woman who never left off plaguing him from the very day of the wedding.

The young folks of the village were not satisfied to stay still, and wait for the day when Stempenyu would go and play at the wedding. The moment that he and his orchestra were well within the village, they boys began to play their pranks. They hid themselves in the corner of the room where all the instruments were piled up, one on top of the other; and, when no one was looking, they came out from their hiding-place, and banged the drum, or pulled the strings of the double-bass. One of the culprits was caught in the act. Yekel Double-bass came on top of him, and gave him a switch with his hand across the neck and shoulders, just as he was bending forward to pull the violin string. Yekel was always cross, and now he was in a perfect fury. He fell upon the boy as if he would tear him to pieces.

While Yekel was dealing with the boy, the village was boiling with excitement. The bridegroom had arrived from his own village, not far away; and, he was accompanied by a number of his relatives and friends. Some dozen or so young men had gone to meet him at the side of the mill, near the spot where the river Yompalle first touches the skirts of the village of Yompalle.

No sooner did the villagers catch sight of the new-comers than they sent up a great shout of welcome, as if the bridegroom had come to rescue them from the hands of a besieging army.

That's how things were in Yompalle; that's how they were in Streista; and that's how they were in all the villages which were so fortunate as to have Stempenyu come into them on great occasions. And, that's how the people showed their joy and enthusiasm in the village of Tasapevka. The people were not so light hearted about the coming of the bridegroom as they made out. The truth was that they did not know what to do with the excitement of having Stempenyu in their midst. They cheered because they had no other way of showing what was going on in their hearts.

But, the villagers had an additional reason beside the coming of Stempenyu to fill them with rejoicing. Red Chayam-Benzion Glock was marrying off his youngest daughter, his baby, Rivkalle. And, the villagers knew that he would make a wedding that would be worth going to; for, he was the wealthiest man in the whole village. He would be sure to give his youngest daughter such a send-off as had never been seen in the village before. And, every single individual was prepared to be present. Some were going out of friendship, some out of jealousy, and some because it was their duty. Nor were there a few among the villagers who were anxious to get the opportunity to show off the jewelry they had bought for their wives at the fair, especially for the occasion. But, they all had in their minds the fact that Stempenyu was going to play at the wedding. The result was that everybody came, filling the house to overflowing.

Isaac-Naphtali and his wife, and son, and daughter-in-law were amongst the first arrivals. For, he was the business partner of Chayam-Benzion, along with being his blood-relation. That is to say, Isaac-Naphtali's wife, Dvossa-Malka, was remotely connected with the wife of Chayam-Benzion, which was the reason why Dvossa-Malka felt so much at home at the wedding. She wore a long veil coming from the front of her head and falling down over her broad shoulders, as if she were the bride's mother; and, she kept wheeling around and about the room, doing nothing at all but gesticulating and making such noises as if everything depended entirely on her. Her daughter-in-law, Rochalle the beautiful, was standing beside the bride, dressed as carefully as if she were a royal princess. Her great blue eyes were shining like lanterns, and her cheeks were like two full blown roses. She was holding the bride's tresses, which the women were braiding together for the last time. Rochalle did not know that a pair of burning black eyes were fixed on her face, never lifting off it for one moment.

The waiters and waitresses were running up and down like frightened hares. The relatives of both parties were so excited that they did nothing but shout aloud at the top of their voices. How long more were they going to carry on the preparations? Surely, it was already time to finish the bride's toilette? Why should she and the bridegroom be kept fasting the whole day? The cry, "It is time! It is time!" became more general, but no one even attempted to do anything whatever. Isaac-Naphtali ran here and there, in a velveteen jacket, under the tails of which he kept his hands locked within each other, as if he were a preacher. And, his wife, Dvossa-Malka, also made a terrible noise, an uproar. Everybody who could ran backwards and forwards, stumbling over one another in their haste, and holding their hands out in front of them, as if they were ready to set to work at anything, but were not given the work to do.

Between the two sets of relations a great rivalry had sprung up; and, two distinct parties were formed, opposing each other at every turn.

"Nu! why is there nothing done yet?" someone belonging to the bridegroom asked, only to be answered by someone from the bride's family with the sneer:

"Why are you not doing something yourself?" And, to this the first speaker made haste to reply: "Did you ever hear the likes? To keep the children fasting for hours and hours on end!"

"Did you ever hear the like—keeping the children fasting for hours and hours on end?" was the opponent's echoing remark.

"Why are they running up and down, here and there?"

"What sort of running about is it?"

"Everybody is running, and everybody is making a noise, and still they are not advancing one step further. Beautiful management!"

"Though they run about and make a noise, they are not doing a single thing."

"Perhaps there is enough talking going on? There must be an end to everything. Let there be a start to get the work done!"

"Well, let there be an end of talking. Let there be a start made to get the work done. There must be an end to this talking."

"Where are the musicians?" asked one of the bride-groom's relatives.

"Yes, the musicians—where are they?" replied the bride's relatives.

The musicians were at this moment occupied in getting themselves ready for the night's work. They were tuning their instruments, and waxing their bows. But, as usual, Yekel Bass was otherwise occupied. He was dragging out of his corner, by the ear, a second delinquent, and dealing him out a goodly share of blows. When he had the boy already outside the door, he whispered, nay, rather hissed into the ear he was pinching with all his might: "I will show you, devil, how to strum the string of my 'bass!' "

Michsa the drummer, not having anything else to do, was scratching the side of his face that had whiskers. He was not looking at anybody. Reb Chaikel Flute was chatting to a teacher of his acquaintance. He took a pinch of snuff from the preacher's box with his forefinger and thumb; and, holding it in mid-air, he proceeded to scatter his words on to the teacher as though he were dropping them from the mouth of a sack.

And, the rest of the musicians—the swollen-faced young man with the long teeth—were standing around Stempenyu, who was talking to them in the jargon that all musicians used, so that no one would understand what they were saying. They seemed to be engrossed in a highly interesting subject.

"Who is the maiden who is standing near the bride?" asked Stempenyu, turning his glances in the direction of Rochalle the beautiful. "You go, Jeremiah," he added, to one of the apprentices, "and find out for me who she is. Be quick about it!"

Jeremiah was not away many minutes. He returned with definite information.

"She is not a maiden. She is a married woman. She is Isaac-Naphtali's daughter-in-law, and comes from Yehupetz. That is her husband in the velvet skull-cap. Do you see him? He is just turning towards us."

"To the devil with you!" cried Stempenyu excitedly. "You were not long finding all this out! Oh, she is very beautiful. Quick! Look at the expression in her wonderful blue eyes!"

"If you wish me to," began the swollen-faced Jeremiah, "if you wish me to, I will start a conversation with her and find out more for you."

"To the devil with you, you hideous monster! Nobody wants you to open your hideous mouth. I can talk to her myself if I want to!"

"Nu!" said someone to Stempenyu, seeing that there was likelihood of a quarrel. "Nu! Stempenyu, make a start. Let them see how you can pierce their hearts with your fiddle; and, how you can tear out their bowels."

Stempenyu needed no further reminder. He took up his fiddle, winked at the men, who at once put themselves in readiness for the signal, and he began to play the opening overture.

No pen can describe how beautifully Stempenyu played the accompaniment to the bride's enthronement. It was not an ordinary wedding march that he played, not by any means an ordinary melody, such as one might have heard anywhere. It was a god-like melody, pervaded with a certain spiritual meaning that was reminiscent of nothing anyone had ever listened to before. It was as if Stempenyu, having taken his stand in front of the bride, was desirous of playing on his fiddle a special sermon for her edification—a long, beautiful sermon touching on the life she had led hitherto, and the different life to which she was going, on the threshold of which she now found herself. Somehow, it seemed that he was particularly anxious to emphasize the contrast between the easy, careless days of maidenhood, and the deep responsibilities which the future held for her. Gone was her childhood, and in its place she would find a serious woman with covered locks, her beauty and her youth hidden under the cap which orthodoxy demanded she should wear. No more joyousness! No more play! No more ease! Farewell youth, farewell! Hail! all hail to the woman that has come forth to the light of day!

Despite the beauty of his playing, the solemnity of it all made it inexpressibly sad. The fiddle seemed to weep and wail after its own fashion, so much so that the women were moved to tears. They could not keep themselves from weeping out loud.

"How short a time it seems since I was a bride myself, sitting on a little throne," murmured an old woman. "It seems but yesterday that I was waiting for the women to tie up my hair. And, I imagined that the angels that are in heaven had intervened in my life; for, it seemed to me that I was the most fortunate creature in the whole wide world. And, how is it in reality? What has it turned out to be?"

"Oh, God," prayed another woman, half aloud. "Oh, God, let it be the fate of my eldest daughter to be married soon. Only let her have better luck than I had. God forgive me for my sinful words!"

While the women were musing thus, Stempenyu was playing. His orchestra now accompanied him at intervals. His fiddle did not play. It talked, saying a multitude of things which were sad, and melancholy to the verge of tears, almost a series of long drawn-out sobs. Not a murmur was to be heard, not a movement. Nothing but the low, thin, plaintive notes of the violin seemed to be in existence. Everybody held his or her breath, for fear of missing a single note. The people felt that it would be better to lose a fortune than a single note from Stempenyu's fiddle. The old men fell into reveries; the women were stricken with dumbness; and the boys and girls clambered on to chairs and tables so as to see the musicians as well as hear them.

And, Stempenyu poured out his soul through the fiddle. He seemed to be melting away out of existence, as if he were wax before a fire. And, now and again, he seemed to come back to earth again, from his soarings in the blue vault of heaven. His thin, fine notes changed to deep, solemn tones that echoed and re-echoed through and through the hearts of his listeners.

A hand flying swiftly up and down—no more than this was to be seen; and yet, one heard all sorts of sweet sounds. A thousand delicious melodies and arias filled the air. And, all of them were so sad that they caught hold of one's heart, and gripped it as with pincers. The people felt that their souls were leaving their bodies. They were dying slowly, inch by inch, their strength drawn out of them by the magic of Stempenyu's playing.

And, who was Stempenyu? What was Stempenyu? No one saw him. No one remembered that he was an individual to himself. And, no one saw the fiddle. One only heard the sweet sounds that came from it—divine voices seemed to be flooding the room with song.

And, Rochalle the beautiful, who had never before heard Stempenyu playing, who had only heard his name, and only knew that such a person as he existed—but who had never heard such music in her life as that which now fell on her ears—Rochalle was standing and listening to the magical tones, the golden harmonies. Did she understand what they conveyed? She did not know what was going on at all. Her heart was filled with something which she had never felt in all her life. She lifted her eyes to the source from which the sweet sounds came, and they encountered a pair of wonderfully beautiful black eyes that burned like living coals. They penetrated her through and through, like sharp daggers. More, they seemed to her eloquent, as if they were filled with the desire to convey to her a special message. She tried to withdraw her eyes from the eyes that were piercing her to her core; but she could not. She was like hypnotized.

"And, so this is Stempenyu!" she thought within herself. But, she got no further than this. There was a sudden movement. The bride was about to be brought under the wedding canopy.

"Where are the candles?" asked one of the bridegroom's relatives.

"The candles—where are they?" was the reply that one of the bride's relatives had to the challenge that had been thrown out.

And, once again there arose the same noise and hubbub which had characterized the beginning of the wedding-day. Everyone took to running here and there, without having the least idea as to why and wherefore of their flight. Everybody was pushing and crushing, and treading on his neighbors' toes. Dresses were torn. And, the people were sweating and abusing the waters and the waitresses, as well as the superintendents, the latter of whom, in turn, abused the guests back again. And, from one end of the room to the other, there passed from lip to lip the sarcastic remark—"Thank goodness, it is a bit lively here!"

In the disorder which prevailed at the time when the bride was being led back from the canopy to her daïs, Stempenyu managed to escape from the orchestra. In a moment, he had reached the spot to which his eyes had wandered a hundred times during the last half-hour, beside the beautiful Rochalle, Isaac-Naphtali's daughter-in-law. He managed to exchange a few words with her, smiling into her blue eyes and showing the agitation which had come upon him by the way in which he kept twirling the stray lock of hair he kept at the side of his forehead. Rochalle blushed scarlet. She feared to look into Stempenyu's eyes, and kept her face averted from him. She hardly knew what he was saying, and only with difficulty managed to say on word to his ten. She felt that it was not all right for a modest young woman to sand talking with a musician before a whole room fell asleep.

Many and various were the tales told of Stempenyu. It was said that he was acquainted with all the magicians, and the "good-folks," and the fairies, and had got from them a certain power which enabled him to do whatever he wished. If he wished to sunder a man from his betrothed, he could do it simply by uttering a certain set of words. And, he only needed to look at a girl, and she would be filled with love for him. It were best, therefore, to take great care of oneself when he was near. As a consequence of his powers, many mothers knew to take care of their daughters. Those of them that were yet unmarried were put under the sheltering wing of their married sisters, or their aunts, or any other married woman who happened to be in the room when Stempenyu was there. It is true that this was no compliment to Stempenyu, but what did that matter? Who is there who would make quarrels when there is peace? Stempenyu's reputation as a musician was not the least bit injured. And, who cared anything beyond that? Nobody was going to marry him, and he remained the same Stempenyu in spite of the fact that many women were afraid of him.

Blessed are the young women who have secured husbands! And, blessed be the men who have secured for their wives freedom! But, alas for the maidens who are bound, and tethered, and guarded, and watched until they have come under the canopy—until they have been freed from their bonds, as happy wives.

As a married woman, Rochalle had nothing to fear from Stempenyu when he came towards her with his fiddle under his arm, and a smile hovering on his lips. What was there to be afraid of? What need for her to hide herself? Her father-in-law, Isaac-Naphtali, was busy with the wedding. He was walking up and down, with his hands hanging loosely by his side. He was scowling at the assistants, and urging them to make haste.

And, her mother-in-law, Dvossa-Malka, was so excited that if anyone had taken her veil off her shoulders she would have known nothing about it. It was true that she did stand up once to see what Stempenyu was doing beside Rochalle. But she did not feel concerned. She said to herself: "What matter! They are only fooling one another. It's not worth half a farthing!"

There were many other things of greater importance than following her son's wife about in a public place. Dvossa-Malka found plenty to do in helping her husband to superintend the arrangements. Between them they managed admirably. The waiters and the waitresses ran about like mad. And, the relatives of both parties made plenty of noise, as usual. The guests went to wash their hands before taking their places at the table, on which there was nothing yet but huge piles of warm rolls. Suddenly there arose an alarm: there was not enough water for all the guests.

"Where are we to get water now?" someone asked.

"Water—yes, where are we to get it now?"

"Water! Water!" shrieked Dvossa-Malka, in a hoarse voice.

"Water! Water!" repeated Isaac-Naphtali, helping to make more noise. He had turned up the tails of his coat, and had begun to believe that he was doing something, whereas he only fussed and flurried everybody.

In the uproar and excitement which prevailed, Stempenyu took advantage of his opportunity, and stayed talking with Rochalle a little longer. She was very thoughtful, and serious. Her beautiful blue eyes had in them a dreamy, far off gaze. She was looking beyond Stempenyu. She listened to him without saying a word, and Stempenyu talked brilliantly. He could talk well, the scamp! His words seemed not only to draw her closer to him but to surround her on all sides, as by a network of invisible silken cords. His eyes were fixed on her face; and, she felt that he was penetrating her through and through, to her very soul, deep, deep down into her heart.

Stempenyu talked, and Rochalle listened, spell bound. And, the noise of the room was so deafening that no one overheard a word of what he was saying.

"Is that your husband?" asked Stempenyu, throwing his eyes in the direction of a young man who was holding the lapel of another man's coat, and arguing with it for all he was worth.

"Yes, that is he," replied Rochalle, walking off from him without ceremony, as if she were offended. And, she felt dimly that he had offended her, though she could not exactly define how, or after what fashion.

Stempenyu fluttered around her still; but she showed him that she had grown tired of him—the same Stempenyu whose glances were so magnetic, and whose personality was so irresistible. She thought that it was wrong for any young woman to so much as stay in the same room with him.

She went back to her place beside the bride, and was ready to forget hat there existed such a person as Stempenyu.

A moment later, a hush fell upon the guests. Stempenyu was again playing a pathetic melody accompanied by the orchestra. Every one was breathless. Every single individual was filled with anxiety lest he or she should lose a note of Stempenyu's playing. Isaac-Naphtali's head drooped to one side, as he listened with the rapt air of a connoisseur. Dvossa-Malka was like rooted to the spot on which she was standing, holding a plate in her hand. And, even the waiters and waitresses were compelled to stand stock-still, enraptured.

And, Stempenyu went on pouring out his soul in the saddest, gloomiest melodies, so that a profound melancholy fell upon everyone who listened to him. They were breathless with the pathos of it all. Their hearts were full, and their tears gushed to their eyes. They wept, and moaned, and sobbed quietly. And Stempenyu? Who was Stempenyu at that moment? What was he? There was no such person as he. There was only a little fiddle, and sweet, yet sad sounds—divine singing that seemed to full the house from roof to cellar.

And, Rochalle the beautiful, who had never before heard Stempenyu playing—she stood now and listened to the enchanting strains—the golden notes the likes of which she had never imagined, much less heard, in all her life. She knew nothing, and understood nothing of what was going on around her. She only knew that her heart was melting within her. She lifted her eyes, and looked up to where the wonderful melody was coming from. And, her eyes encountered Stempenyu's black eyes fixed on her face, piercing her to the core, like dagger thrusts. At the same time, the piercing eyes were pleading with her, beckoning to her, speaking to her in seductive terms.

Rochalle dropped her eyes; but, she knew that the burning eyes were still fixed on her. She felt uncomfortable and hot, and tried to turn out of the way of the burning eyes; but, they were still following her with their haunting expression, their supplications, their pleadings.

VI AFTER THE SUPPER

The wedding supper was long over. The people were making merry, dancing and laughing, and eating and drinking. Each of the guests took it in turn to pay for a dance; but, it was always the liveliest dance. Yontel the Butcher called for a *Cossak's* dance, and the brides' mother stepped out in front of him, quickly and bravely. A loud applause went up. And, Yontel was so hot and excited that he did not see he was really dancing opposite to a woman, and not a man as he imagined; for, he never suspected that any woman would be so immodest as to step out, and dance in front of him.

The bride's mother was smiling at him—a broad, good-natured smile that covered the whole of her broad face, so that she looked like the full moon.

The dancing soon became general. Isaac-Naphtali had taken off his long coat, and was in his shirt-sleeves.

He had been laughed at the whole evening because of the way he kept his coat tucked up, until he felt compelled to take it off. Someone pushed a big hat over his nose, and the whole roomful of people roared at him, boisterously and carelessly, having tasted freely of the strong liquor which had been provided. Even his own son, Moshe-Mendel, Roshalle's husband, was pulling his father by the sleeve into the corner, as he cried: "Jump to the ceiling, jump to the ceiling, everybody!"

The musicians were now playing by themselves. Stempenyu had left them to go and mingle with the crowd. He was as gay and as noisy as any of them.

The leadership of the orchestra was in the hands of one of the young men with the long teeth. Shneyer-Meyer, the second fiddle, had dozed off, and Yekel Double-bass was fast asleep. But, the younger men were playing for all they were worth, Michsa Drummer working like a galley-slave to make up the deficiency of the instruments. He felt like a murderer, vicious towards his drum as if it were the most hateful thing in the whole world. He hid his yellow head behind the drum. He seemed to have vanished out of sight, excepting for his shoulders, which showed out above the drum, and his feet, which beat time on the floor.

Meanwhile, Stempenyu was fluttering around the young women, keeping near to Rochalle most of the time.

"Let us go home," said Rochalle to her mother-in-law, who was staring at her husband with the big hat on his nose, and his arms in his shirt-sleeves.

"Come, my daughter, come," she replied. "You are right. It is time to go home. To-morrow is market-day, and we must rise early. See how they are enjoying themselves!"

Dvossa-Malka went home with Rochalle.

The dark blue sky had a patch of lighter shade on one side. It was the dawn breaking through the clouds of night. A cock crowed somewhere, and a dozen others took up the cry. Far away in the distance, a dog was barking. But, not a soul was yet astir. Even the field laborers were still fast asleep in their tiny huts. The only house that showed signs of life was the one which was inhabited by an old Jew who was in the habit of reading for an hour before he set out on his daily tasks.

"What do you say to Nathan's daughter, Rochalle? Has she not grown in the width? Do you like her?" But, Rochalle was silent. She had not heard what was said. She was deeply engrossed in her own reflections. Who can say what or about whom she was thinking?

"Aunt," she said, addressing her mother-in-law, to whom she sometimes gave that name, "I heard Stempenyu playing for the first time in my life to-night!"

"Go away, child! For the first time in your life?" was the answer. "Didn't he play at Reb Leib-Abram's? And what about the wedding of Sarah Benzion's daughter? And what about the wedding of Reb himself?"

"I do not remember," said Rochalle. "I only remember hearing people repeat the name of Stempenyu again and again; but, I do not think I ever saw him before."

"Nu, that's to be understood. At the time I speak of you were no more than—let me see—how old could you have been then? You were only a tiny child when Stempenyu played at the Rebbe's wedding in the village of Skvirro. Oh, what a wedding that was! May all my best friends get married after the same grand fashion, with the help of the Almighty! That was before my poor twins were born. But where are you going to, Rochalle? Here is our house, and you passed it by, in the moment when I did not notice where you were taking me."

"Did you ever see the like?" cried Rochalle, looking about her in some confusion. "Did you ever hear the like?" she repeated, and burst out laughing.

And, she was still laughing when they entered the house.

They both went to bed without the least delay, anxious to get a few hours sleep before having to get up to go to the market on the morrow. This market was one of the few big ones which took place ion Tasapevka during the year. It was almost a fair.

Did you ever hear the likes? Without having the least cause to account for it, Rochalle cannot fall asleep. She keeps twisting, and turning, and covering herself, and uncovering herself; but, no sleep comes to her. She tries her best to drive him out of her mind—Stempenyu, I mean, of course. But, he still stood before her eyes, goodness alone knew why. She closed her eyes tightly, but, she saw him just as clearly. She found herself compelled to haze back into the burning eyes that were staring at her out of the darkness, beckoning to her, and pleading with her.

"Oh, I wish I could stop thinking of him! Oh, if only Moshe-Mendel were here!" she moaned piteously. And, when she opened her eyes again, it was only to imagine they rested on the full length figure of Stempenyu, who was standing before her with his fiddle in his hand. And, once again, she found herself listening to his wondrous playing! And, oh, what sweet music it was! Surely, it was not altogether without reason that such awe-inspiring tales were told of him?

As she lay there in the darkness and the silence, all the stories she had heard about him long ago, when she was a child, now came back to her with full force. She remembered distinctly the time she was learning to write at the school kept by my Mottel Sprais, the girls' teacher. She first heard the name of Stempenyu, sitting in a desk, surrounded by a number of other girls of her own age. They were talking between themselves of how Stempenyu had enticed a young woman away from her betrothed; and, how, for grief and shame, the young woman had died of a broken heart, and had had a black wedding ceremony made after her, instead of the usual joyful ceremony. The girls went on telling how Stempenyu had taken his revenge against a girl who called him a charlatan; and, how he had refused the hand of a noblewoman's daughter—a woman of remarkable beauty. The moment this beautiful woman had laid eyes on Stempenyu, she had fallen madly in love with him. She declared that she must get him, even if she were to die in the attempt. When the nobleman had heard that his daughter was madly in love with Stempenyu, and that she would die if she did not get him, he went at once to Stempenyu, and threatened him with all sorts of terrible things if he did not marry his daughter at once. But, Stempenyu was not at all frightened. He refused to listen to any such proposal. So, the nobleman tried to win him for his daughter by another method. He began to persuade him in the kindest of terms, and even promised him for dowry three villages, if he would only consent to marry his daughter, who was dying of love for him. But, Stempenyu replied to him in French (he knew both French and German thoroughly), that even if he filled his house with gold pieces, he would not change his religion, nor marry the beautiful noblewoman. And, ever since that day Stempenyu has been the greatest favourite with all the Jews he ever came across, including even the Rabbis themselves. They feel that he has a true Jewish heart, whatever his faults.

And, as for the beautiful noblewoman—when she heard what Stempenyu had said, she jumped into the river, and was drowned.

Such were the stories which had been told of Stempenyu in all the little villages. They believed him to be at once the greatest genius, and the most heartless wretch that had ever existed, in spite of the good he sometimes brought about by his sharpness and his wit. And, when the girls told each other about Stempenyu, a shiver ran through them. How well Rochalle could recall her feelings! And alas! how the stories had haunted her for days afterwards.

But, above everything else, Rochalle had been impressed with the stories that were told of Stempenyu and his love-philtre. As she went over everything, she was struck by the worthlessness of love and love philters. No love-philtre was worth a single farthing! "In our own way, my Moshe-Mendel and I love one another, and neither of us ever saw a philter of any sort in our lives."

Rochalle turned over on her side with her face to the wall, and went on thinking of everything just as before. "Surely," she thought, "I love Moshe-Mendel! At any rate, I do not dislike him!"

But, after all, why should she dislike him? He was not an ugly young man. And, he was inclined to be modern. He wore his earlocks under his hat, and read the newspaper, and recited his prayers beautifully, and was always ready to exchange witticisms with the old people, and to play practical jokes with the young men. Altogether, he was a fine and worthy specimen of a man, and any woman might be proud of him. On the other hand, it was equally true that he often behaved toward Rochalle as if he were a savage. And, he hardly ever spoke two whole thoughts to her unless he must. One word was enough. She had to be satisfied with the shortest explanation of anything. He gave her an order to do this or that, and the next minute he was off out of the house, either to the House of Learning, or else to the market-place. He never dreamt of sitting down to talk to her in a friendly way. Nor did he ever ask her opinion or her feeling about anything. And, certainly he never would listen to any argument that his wife might bring forward on any subject under the sun. He was as a wild goat.

This was not at all the treatment that Rochalle had looked forward to on her betrothal to him. Indeed, so happy had she felt in being his bride that she believed in her heart that every girl envied her for her good fortune in getting him for a husband. She felt quite sure that there was not anyone to equal Moshe-Mendel in the whole wide world. He was so handsome, in her eyes, so good, so clever, so cultured. It was impossible to find another Moshe-Mendel amongst the ordinary folks of the earth. Perhaps his likes might be found amongst those good old folks who live in the Heavenly Paradise. And, oh, how happy all this made her!

And, what was the end of everything? How had her hopes been justified? She saw now that the very girls whose envy she thought she had excited because of her betrothal to Moshe-Mendel—they were all happy, whilst she was altogether different from what she had expected. One girl had gone with her husband to live in a large city, from which she was writing home the best of news in letters that gave one pleasure to read, even. Another was very happy in her modest home in a village. And, even Chana-Mirrel, who had married a widower with five children, and had by this put her whole future into one venture—she, too, was as happy as she desired to be. And, what could she say when it came to her turn to be criticized? She had nothing to say for herself. Her whole life was empty. The whole week round, she ate, drank, and slept, and felt every hour of the day how like she was to the little birds that are kept in cages,, and are given everything their hearts could desire, but can never go free, can never break the bars of their cages. She was nothing at all to Moshe-Mendel. His walks, and his smart sayings, and his companions were much more to him than was Rochalle.

A loud knocking at the door broke up the chain of her musings. It was Moshe-Mendel coming home from the wedding. His mother got up, and opened the door for him.

"Moshe-Mendel!"

"Well, What?"

"Is that you, Moshe-Mendel?" asked his mother from the other side of the door.

But, Moshe-Mendel was too confused to answer her

question. His reply was: "Nu, another dance—this one. B-r-r-r!"

"What are you jabbering about? Take off your clothes, and get into bed."

"We had a good drink his time—hadn't we, Berel-Menaseeh—eh? A good sup?"

"God be with you, Moshe-Mendel, whatever are you talking about?" cried Dvossa-Malka to him, as she struck a match.

"Aunt, can't you see that he is dead drunk?" put in Rochalle. "Please light a candle for him, or he will break his neck in the dark."

"No such thing! Another little glass!" With these words, Moshe-Mendel flung himself across the bed, and was fast asleep, snoring loudly before the two women had time to realize anything. Dvossa-Malka went back to bed too, and the house was wrapped in silence once more, except for Moshe-Mendel's snoring.

The wind was whistling, and blowing down the chimney, and sighing softly as it tore around the wooden walls, the breeze sounded and resounded until it was as loud as a storm. Everyone else in the house was fast asleep—only Rochalle lay awake listening to the wind moaning and sobbing. She could not fall asleep, and was glad to have the pencil like rays of the moon to distract her from Stempenyu. The light falling through the window gave her something to look at—showed up to her the form of her husband lying on the bed, his face upwards, his mouth wide open, his eyes fixed in a glassy stare, and his bare, knotty throat showing ugly in the brilliant moonlight.

Rochalle turned away from the sight of her husband. She did not wish to look at him, and yet she could do nothing else. Her eyes turned on him again and again, despite her wishes to the contrary. And, as she looked at him, she realized that he had never before seemed so hately to her as he was now.

But, along with having a changed feeling for Moshe-Mendel, she was conscious of the fact that she kept comparing him, unwittingly, with someone by the side of whom he was less than a nobody. She was comparing him with the good-for-nothing Stempenyu, who seemed to tower over him by several heads and shoulders. And, each moment, she found new faults in her husband, and new virtues in Stempenyu; so that she could hardly believe she had really been led into imagining that Moshe-Mendel was even an ordinary man, much less the noble being she had taken him for.

Where now were the charms, the pleasant manners, and the wit she had seen in him? Where was his beauty gone, and his youthful joyous bearing? What had become of the glowing words and the expressive gestures about which she had gone into raptures? Could this be really the same Moshe-Mendel of only a short little while back? No, no; he was not the same. He had changed beyond recognition. And, everything was changed along with him.

And, in place of her husband, the vision of Stempenyu stood before her to harass her, and to bring down the ridicule upon Moshe-Mendel. She could not shake herself free from the vision, however much she tried—she could not. She was caught fast in the toils of her own imagination.

Away, away, dark temptation, from the heart and mind of this pure soul—this Jewish woman whose innocent heart is far from guile!

Next morning, when Chana, the beadle's wife, came to Dvossa-Malka's house to tell her that the bride and bridegroom, and all the relatives and friends of both parties, wished her and her husband, and their son, and his wife to come to the wedding-breakfast, Rochalle was already dressed in her best gown, which was of pale blue silk and had been made by the famous tailor, David. It had large puffed out sleeves, and white silk bows. The fashion of it was just new to Tasapevka, though it had gone out of date elsewhere three years before. On her head, she wore a blue silk cap of Oriental design, through which might have been seen the neat plaits of her golden hair, her beautiful curls which she kept hidden away out of sight. She had several rows of pearls around her beautiful neck, and wore a long gold chain, a brooch, earrings and finger-rings. In short, the whole set of ornaments which were fashionable amongst the Jewish women of her day.

Being fully dressed, she was sitting in the best room of the house. And, she was listening to the snores of Moshe-Mendel, who was still sleeping in exactly the same position. His head was thrown back, his eyes were glazed, and his mouth was wide open. His long bony neck showed still more hideously than even it had in the moonlight. Rochalle sighed as she listened to the regular rhythm of his loud snores. And, she went on with the thoughts which had vexed her the night before. She went over the same ground, in an undertone.

"Oh, what a difference there is in you, Moshe-Mendel, to whom I betrothed myself not so long ago. That time you were so charming, and had such bright eyes. They seemed to dance themselves into my heart. Your glances were like flames to me. They enkindled all the passions that were within me. Everything about you was so charming, so fascinating, and so lovable! And what are you now, Moshe-Mendel? You are an altogether different man. You were slender and graceful then; now you are hideously long and skinny. Your little yellow whiskers are only fit to be cut off this minute. Wherever did you get such a beard?"

And again, without wishing it, Rochalle held up the good-for-nothing Stempenyu for a model of perfection, by the side of whom her Moshe-Mendel was only a poor scarecrow. She forgot that Stempenyu had haunted her all the night, so tat she had not slept a wink.

"It is a great misfortune. But, I alone am to blame for it," she thought, "I alone am to blame. The moment the good-for-nothing Stempenyu sands up before me, I talk to him, as if it were quite an ordinary thing to talk to a musician. What will the villagers say about me? It was well there was such a noise and uproar at the wedding. What would Moshe-Mendel say if he knew?"

She got up and went into the bedroom. She smiled grimly as she bent over her husband, and called him by his name. He opened his grey eyes, and stared blankly about him. It was some little time before he realized where he was, and who was bending over him.

"Moshe-Mendel," said Rochalle, bending still lower over him; "Moshe-Mendel, do you not know me? You look as if you were amazed to find me here. Tell me how you like my new bonnet and veil?"

"Oh, leave me alone. I want to sleep." With these words Moshe-Mendel turned over on his side, and was soon fast asleep, and snoring loudly once more.

"The bride and bridegroom, and the parents and the friends of both parties, sent me to tell you that they are expecting you and your husband, and your father and mother-in-law, to come at once to the wedding breakfast."

Chana called out the message as she popped her head inside the bedroom door; for, she found that all the other rooms in the house were empty. But, catching sight of Rochalle as she was bending over her sleeping husband, Chana withdrew in the greatest confusion, and rushed off in hot haste.

* * *

When Rochalle arrived, the bride was still wearing her wedding garments. The two young women kissed each other, and at once started to talk in rapid voices, after the fashion of all young women who have much to say to one another.

The guests began to fill the house, and the waiters and waitresses loaded the tables with all manner of dainties. The superintendents, all the poor people who had been invited out of charity, were already in their places. The bride's father, Chayam-Benzion, was running about here and there, in a velvet skull-cap, and a new coat; and the bride's mother was already so hoarse that no one could make out a word of what she was saying. But, she persisted in trying to make order. She drove one person here and the other there; and, she shouted with all her might.

"Do you want to ruin me?" she cried to the waiters. "You go and place a dish of tarts on the table when you should have whisky and sponge-cake there. Woe is me! Ah, woe is me! Can I tear myself to pieces? There's a wedding gift for you! It cost us a pile of money, and what is there for it? Even the musicians take advantage of me! They are not here yet. The cheek of them! As if they had anything else to do but put on their clothes, and hurry over here at once!"

"Shah! Let there be piece!" put in Chayam-Benzion. "What are you raving about? What good are you doing by roaring? You are doing nothing but adding to the terrible noise. Is it anything new to you to marry off a daughter? One would imagine that the like had never happened to you before. The whole town has come to the wedding, and you stand there roaring with your mouth wide open. And why are you roaring—I should like to know?"

"Who is roaring, mad animal, who is roaring?"

"I know who is roaring. Say yourself, who is roaring?"

"I am not roaring. You are roaring."

"I am roaring? No, it is just the opposite."

"Now you are roaring. Chayam-Benzion, what has come over you to make you so spiteful? Tell me that."

"A good morning to all—to bride and groom, and all the relatives, friends, and well-wishers! Vivat!"

With these words, Chaikel the flute player led in the rest of the orchestra, all of whom took their places without any more ado. And, in a few moments, the rejoicings were again in full swing. The guests made a wild rush to secure the best places at the tables.

Stempenyu took his fiddle in his hand, and once more the roomful of people were spell-bound by his music. He replayed all the melodies he had played last night, but, with many additions and variations. He also played several new pieces, to which everybody listened with bated breath. Every eye was fixed on Stempenyu's face; and, every face was drawn and pale from excitement. Only Rochalle kept her head averted so as not to meet the burning eyes of Stempenyu. At the same time, she managed to catch a glimpse of him, now and again. It was not until he had finished, and had laid aside his fiddle, and gone amongst the guests, that she ventured to lift up her blue eyes towards his face.

"What do you think of him?" asked the bride, who had up till that moment kept silent.

"What do I think of whom?" asked Rochalle, feigning ignorance.

"Of Stempenyu, of course. They say he is a fine scamp!"

Rochalle did not answer her. But, that did not prevent her from blushing scarlet. The bride noticed her change of color, and asked if she felt hot.

"Oh, yes, it is very hot in this room. I will go out into the air to cool myself." And, Rochalle left the room. At every step, she stumbled up against a man or woman carrying this or that. And, each person bowed low before Rochalle; but, not so much for her own sake as because of her beautiful silk mantle.

She did not reach the door at once; for, first of all, she had to pass the musicians who eyed her sharply, and made remarks about her in their own jargon which she somehow understood without explanation. "What a lovely woman!" they said. "I should like to have a chat with her. She's perfection itself."

When her eyes met those of Stempenyu, she experienced a peculiar contraction of the heart. And, her pulse beat more quickly that it had beaten in all her life. The colour again mounted to her cheeks; and, she felt as hot as if she had just managed to escape from a burning house.

In the effort she made to escape from Stempenyu, she almost ran into Chayam-Benzion, who was flustered and excited by the little encounter. He was a Jew of almost unbending piety, and never wished to come face to face with any woman whatever whom he could possibly avoid. It seemed to him that all sinful thoughts and temptations were connected only with the female sex. When he came upon Rochalle, he felt that he ought to turn his back on her immediately, without any regard for the fact that she might think him rude; but, he did not turn from her at all. He walked in her direction for a few steps; then, thinking better of it, he turned away from her, and took the opposite direction from that she was going. Seeing he was going to the left, Rochalle, wishing to avoid him, too the right-hand side of the way. And, he, seeing that she was taking the right, grew confused and went on a little with her. She, seeing he was going to the right, wheeled round to the left.

And, they might have gone dodging each other for goodness knows how long, without getting out of the tangle in the least, if his wife had not called out to him in her croaking, hoarse voice to say that she was waiting for him to come and dance with her.

And, at last, Rochalle managed to get into the open air.

But, Rochalle found that the open air was hardly any cooler out of doors than indoors. It was a hot July day. The sun was high in the heavens. Its rays were scorching and burning everything up without mercy. The straw roofs of the tiny cottages reflected the rays in a thousand brilliant sparks of light of all possible shades and colour. The sunbeams sparkled and rippled on the surface of the river, and they were beautiful to look upon. The boys of the village called this dancing sunbeam by the name of the "Divine Presence," meaning thereby that it was an almost unearthly thing, and had in it something holy, and pure, and exceptional.

Over against where Rochalle was standing was the market square of Tasapevka, now silent and deserted. At the furthest side of the square a long row of booths and little shops spread out their red awnings to the morning sun. At the doors of the tiny edifices, on low, four legged stools, sat the market women, knitting socks with great rapidity, the steel needles flashing in the sun like little daggers. Some of the women had their wares set out on little tables beside them—set forth as temptingly as possible, so that any passerby might be drawn to purchase some of the little tarts, or the shiny berries, or the little buns that were filled with currants.

A goat was wandering in and out of the booths and the little shops, bent on doing as much mischief as she could. But her career was cut short. She was driven off by the women with shouting and the shaking of large aprons at her.

In the distance, there might have been seen coming towards the village a huge cart drawn by two oxen fresh from the plough. The cart was laden with corn-stalks, and it rumbled, and rattled, and shook, as it lumbered slowly over the uneven road, the wheels falling into ruts over and over again. Underneath the cart ran a little peasant boy in a big hat, carrying a bag in his hand. He was barefooted, and as he ran, he cracked a whip at the dog that was running around him with his tongue lolling out, and breathing heavily.

Rochalle stood for a while contemplating the scene that was before her. The commonplace rusticity of it all was not to her liking. She turned her thoughts to her own superiority—her fine clothes and her jewels. And, she felt that she was, in reality, far removed from everybody and everything around her. And, at the same time she realized that she was not definitely better than anyone else. She was neither one thing nor another—neither a market woman nor a great lady. She was, after all, an ordinary middle-class woman who neither feared to become a market woman, nor had the least hopes of ever becoming a great lady. She could never be a real peasant woman, any more than she could be a princess. She was married to a man whose father had provided them both with everything, so that there was not the least need for her to put her fingers into cold water. And, her husband spent his days between the House of Learning and the market square. He did nothing but go about, stick in hand, telling stories and cracking jokes.

Now, as she found herself face to face with the primitive life about her, she began to realize who and what she was. It came strikingly before her, for the first time in her life, that she wanted something. She could not even guess of what nature that something was. She only knew that there was a want within her. She did not question herself. She knew that she had hit upon a profound truth. And, she looked back on herself and her whole life, and found that she was only an ordinary girl—a daughter of the Jewish people. She was neither sharp, nor clever, nor well-educated. She had grown up amongst a lot of other children, and her parents had never petted her nor made much of her.

"She is only a girl," they said. "Let her grow up strong. That's all we ask of her, or expect."

And, in order that they might have one burden the less on their shoulders, one child less playing about the house, Rochalle had been sent to school with the boys. When she grew a little older, they sent her to learn to write from old Mottel Sprais, who kept a school for girls. She made many friends amongst the girls she found at the school. She liked best to sit with the older girls, and to listen to the stories they used to tell one another. She always thought their stories were beyond compare for wonder, and excitement. And, the girls in turn loved the little Rochalle for her gentle ways; but, more especially for her clear, melodious voice. A dozen times a day someone said to her:

"Sing us something, Rochalle. There is no one near us. The boys have gone away to play elsewhere."

Rochalle was ashamed to sing if there was anyone near her. She did not mind the girls; but, she was shy before the older people or the boys. The girls themselves told her it was not nice to sing when the big boys were within hearing distance. It was forbidden, besides.

"Well, sing for us. How many times have we to ask you, Rochalle?"

And, Rochalle obeyed the girls, and began to sing, in her thin, childish, but pleasant, voice, a little Yiddish song, a doggerel verse something like this:

> "On the hill stands a dove,
> Softly sighing and moaning—
> 'Far-off is my love,
> Far off is he roaming!' "

Rochalle sang the love-song with much feeling. It was as if she understood already, at her age, the meaning of the word "love." But, the others, the girls who were listening to her, understood the meaning of the word much better than she did. They sighed as she sang, and often shed tears as well. One of the girls in particular loved to hear Rochalle sing. She was an orphan girl of great beauty, whose name was Chaya-Ettel. Her history was brief, nor was it in any respect singular. Indeed, so common are histories like hers, that one could tell them in a breath without the least fear of being misunderstood.

Several years before Chaya-Ettel's introduction into this history, there lived two brothers in the same village. One brother was called Aaron, and the other was Leib. Aaron was quite a young man when he died, and his wife did not long survive him. They left behind them a little child, Chaya-Ettel. Her uncle Leib was full of pity for the tiny orphan, and he took her, and adopted her—along with her inheritance. He did not treat her well. But, he kept a tight hold of her inheritance, which, according to the report that was current in the village, amounted to no less than three thousand *roubles*. The very moment he could, he married Chaya-Ettel to the first-comer, a man who was altogether wanting in character and principle. He treated her so harshly that Chaya-Ettel could not live over his treatment. She died at the early age of twenty-two, of a broken heart.

When she was still a child, and went to the school of Mottel Sprais to learn to write, she grew very much attached to Rochalle. They were never apart, and their love never waned.

One Sabbath morning, when the two little girls were sitting in the window-seat, both of them dressed in their best clothes, Rochalle began to sing, while Chaya-Ettel listened:

> "Ah, you are going away—
> Ah, you are going away,
> And me you are leaving behind!"

"Rochalle, my darling, my love, sing that again," Chaya-Ettel begged of her.

"Very well, I will begin it again if you wish.

> "Ah, you are going away—
> Ah, you are going away,
> And me you are leaving behind!"

Chaya-Ettel was completely overcome. She fell forward, buried her face in her hands, and wept bitterly, her whole body heaving with agitation.

"God help you, Chaya-Ettel, are you weeping? Why are you weeping? Tell me what was come over you that you bust out weeping all at once?"

"Oh, Rochalle," she managed to say at last, "it is your song—your little song."

"My little song? What is there in it to make you weep?"

"Oh, Rochalle, do not ask me. Do not ask to me to tell you all that is in my embittered heart. A fire is burning within me—a terrible fire. Just here I feel it—just here, near my heart?"

Chaya-Ettel put her hand to her heart, and Rochalle looked at her in bewilderment, and amazement.

"Why do you look at me so, Rochalle? You do not understand what I am suffering. You can never understand what goes on within me. My heart feels as heavy as lead; and, I am so lonely, and so miserable. I carry about with me a load of sorrow. But, I will tell you everything—everything.

Chaya-Ettel proceeded to tell Rochalle a whole story which one may hear from any Jewish man or woman almost any day of the week; but, a sad story for all that. She told Rochalle of the death of her two parents within a short time of one another; and how, since the day on which her uncle had taken her into his own house, she had suffered all sorts of ill-treatment. Her uncle was unkind to her, it was true; but her aunt was worse by far. And, had it not been for her uncle's younger son, Benjamin, she would have run away long ago. More than this, she might have drowned herself in the river. Benjamin was so good to her that he consoled her almost entirely for what she had to suffer every day of the week. They had grown up together, and were more like sister and brother than cousins. But, at the end of some time, he went away, and left her all alone amongst total strangers; that is to say, not real strangers, but relatives who were worse to her than if they had been the blackest of black strangers.

"I don't see why one should weep when a friend goes away," remarked Rochalle. "Even if he was to you a real broker, and he was not, you need not break your heart after him, nor cry your eyes out!"

"Oh, Rochalle, you do not know how kind he was to me. And, his image is as deeply rooted in my heart as if he had really been my brother. Nay, even more than if he had been of my own flesh and blood. I tell you, Rochalle, when I saw Benjamin it was as if a candle had been lit in the darkness. Everything was bright. And when he went away—"

"Benjamin had to go away, had he not? Didn't he get married?"

"Oh, Rochalle, do not mention it. I hate the word, 'married.' It seems to take the very life from me. When they tell me that Benjamin is married, it seems to me that the end of my days has come. You know nothing of such things, Rochalle, and I hope you never will. But, why do you look at me in such a curious way? Benjamin promised that he would marry me. He swore it!"

Nu! And what if he did not marry you, Chaya-Ettel?"

"You talk like a child, Rochalle. It was not my fate. It was another girl's destiny to be so lucky as to marry him!"

"But, had he not sworn to marry you?"

"Well, and if he did swear it? He was always promising to ask his father's permission; but, he kept putting it off from day to day. You know what sort of a man my uncle is? Benjamin was afraid to approach him. And, one day, he found himself betrothed to her. I talked to him about it; and, he made answer, hat as the day of the wedding is still far off, there was yet time for him to talk to his father. And, in this way, the weeks and the months flew by. And, the wedding day came round. I myself stood beside the canopy when they were married. With my own eyes I saw how they put the ring on her finger; and, with my own ears, I heard them pronounce the blessing. The Cantor and his choir sang a loud, joyful hymn. Benjamin drooped his eyes on to the floor, so that he might avoid meeting my eyes. But, I know that he saw me all the same. Oh, Rochalle, how can I live over all these miseries? How can I stand them all?"

"In that case, Chaya-Ettel, Benjamin is a great liar, and is not worth the ground he stands on."

"No, Rochalle, I tell you he is no liar. You do not know him. You have no idea what a diamond he is. He has a most loving heart. No one but my uncle is to blame for it all—he alone—the tyrant! May my dead father rise up and take revenge of him. Oh, lord, may the wrath of heaven come upon him!"

"I can see, Chaya-Ettel, that your pain is great!"

"Pain? I am dying. My strength is going from me! And, she calls it pain!"

"And she, Chaya-Ettel, is she a beautiful woman?"

"Is who a beautiful woman?"

"She—Benjamin's wife, I mean."

At these words Chaya-Ettel turned red as fire, and then became pale as death. She was all colours, as the phrase has it. Rochalle could not understand why she remained silent, refusing to answer the question. But, she felt instinctively that she ought to let it pass without repeating it. She thought that Chaya-Ettel did not wish to make any remarks about the woman who had ousted her. She had no doubt that it would pain her to speak of the affair any more.

* * *

Long afterwards, Rochalle came upon Chaya-Ettel at a wedding—her own wedding, in fact. And, to Rochalle she was a bride just like any other bride—very still, and silent, and agitated.

Next day, after having sat amongst the guests who had been feasting in her honour all the night, Chaya-Ettel took off all her finery, her wedding-dress, and her veil, and everything else which she had to wear as a bride, and gave herself up to resignation. She was pale as death, and a good deal abstracted; but, that did not matter. Nor did it seem to matter that she was not at all joyful, as she ought to have been. She thought bitterly that everything was as it should be. Surely, no one could expect her to dance, and sing, and hop about like a bird on her wedding?

But it was evident that her heart was full of emotion. Who can tell what her real feelings were? The heart of a Jewish woman is a secret. It is as a box to which no one has a key. No one may see into it. And, according to the traditions which are so strongly adhered to in the villages and towns of the Russian Pale, it is neither seemly nor desirable that any man should concern himself with the heart of a woman. It is as if she had no heart, and no secrets buried in it.

Rochalle mused long on the question of what Chaya-Ettel must be thinking of on the day of her wedding. Rochalle made no remark to anybody, nor did she ask a single question. But, her own sense told her that there must be something very unusual taking place in Chaya-Ettel's heart. She was certainly not in the best form, as she sat beside the man whom her uncle had destined for her mate, but who was a complete stranger to her. All the more must she have been filled with emotions of a conflicting nature because of the fact that Benjamin and his wife seemed to have gone out of her life altogether. But, Rochalle believed that Chaya-Ettel was in reality thinking of Benjamin now, at the very moment when she ought to have been thinking of no one else but the man who was now her husband.

Rochalle would have liked to ask her what she had

heard last from Benjamin, or if she had heard anything at all. She drew closer to the bride in order to ask the question; but, when she saw how pale she was, and heard her sighing to herself, Rochalle could not find it in her heart to gratify her curiosity—to ask her anything about Benjamin.

Hitherto, Rochalle felt and understood and knew very little about life itself. She had never come into contact with anything which might have struck a deep chord in her heart. But, she was stirred to the depths now by the very same facts of life which had hitherto left her unstirred. Though she was only an ordinary, commonplace girl, without education, she was not a fool. She understood what was going on around her. It was true also that she knew nothing of the heroes and romances. But, she had a clear conscience, and a pure heart; and therefore, she could sympathize readily with another's grief and pain. She felt that she herself was filled with the sorrow which vexed the heart of her friend.

On the moment when she caught the first glimpse into the workings of Chaya-Ettel's heart, Rochalle seemed to have added many years to her age—ten years at the very least. Thanks to the knowledge she had of Chaya-Ettel's unhappy attachment, Rochalle was an old woman, thought she had been a fresh young creature only a little while before.

At that time, at the time when she was attended Chaya-Ettel's wedding, Rochalle was herself already betrothed to Moshe-Mendel, of whom she had heard so much, whose praises were sung so frequently and by so many mouths that she began to look upon herself as the luckiest girl in the whole world.

"What luck!" they cried. "May no Evil Eye interfere to upset her happiness. She has come upon a valley of fatness! How on earth did she manage to lay hold of him? His father, Isaac-Naphtali, is the foremost Jew of all the Jews of Tasapevka. And, Moshe-Mendel himself is an only child. And, what a son he is, what a son! There's luck for you!"

And, in truth, Moshe-Mendel was a nice young man whom anyone could like. He was pleasant, and clever, and smart. He knew a good deal of the Talmud, and his witty sayings were taken up and repeated and handed round, so to speak, from one end of the village to the other. He wrote so well, such a beautiful hand, that even Mottel Sprais himself, the girls' teacher, who was certainly the best writer in the district—even he was compelled to take note of Moshe-Mendel's calligraphy. One day the old man saddled his nose with his silver-rimmed spectacles, and examined closely and carefully the specimen of Moshe-Mendel's handwriting which had been submitted to him for approval. He did his best to find fault with it; but, in the end, he had to admit that Moshe-Mendel could lay some claim to the possession of the great ideal—"a golden hand," as the old phrase had it. But, Mottel-Sprais took good care to qualify his praise. He expressed the opinion that Moshe-Mendel was certainly clever; and that, in the course of time, with much practice, if God willed, he would be able to write fairly well. He was promising in that direction.

Rochalle had not much chance of finding out for herself the good qualities of Moshe-Mendel. But, then, how could she when she had so little opportunity of coming face to face with him? He remained in his village, in

Tasapevka, and she in hers, Yehupetz, which was several miles off. And they had seen each other only once, and then in the presence of a whole houseful of people, for a couple hours. She was in one part of the room, and he in the other, so that they could hardly say with truth they knew what they each looked like—she in his eyes, and he in hers. But, for that again, they wrote to each other regularly once a week for a whole year, until they were married. What is the use in denying the truth? Mottel Sprais took a large part in Rochalle's letter-writing; for, Moshe-Mendel's letters were written so well, and in three languages—Hebrew, Russian, and German—that Rochalle was compelled to ask the help of Mottel Sprais in answering. She had no wish to show her ignorance. Mottel was more than willing to help her. He wished to let the whole world know that from his school the girls did not come out ignorant dunces, as happened in the case of other schools. In fact, he was so eager to advance the merits of his school that he did not scruple to add to the letter he wrote at Rochalle's dictation many French words, to show that he knew the French language as well as the German.

In short, one might say that for a whole year Moshe-Mendel and Rochalle did nothing else but write letters to one another. They only left off when they were about to go under the wedding canopy.

The wedding came off in the usual fashion, which means that the relatives on both sides grumbled a good deal about the way this and that was managed. Each one said that there was too much selfishness shown. And the bridegroom's people went so far as to call the bride's father the name of an unclean animal that is forbidden by

Jewish law. But, when the wedding was completely at an end, they forgave one another freely, and parted the best of friends, each set of families going its way in peace.

A few days afterwards, Rochalle drove off from her father's house to the village of Tasapevka to take up her residence with her husband and his parents.

There in her new home, Rochalle began an entirely new life. Rochalle, the wife of their only child, and the beautiful Rochalle that she was besides, at once won the hearts of every person with whom she came into contact. But, she was the particular favourite of Moshe-Mendel's parents. They took care of her, and kept guard over her every hour of the day, lest so much as a speck of dust fall on her.

Dvossa-Malka, who had counted the days until her son should bring home a wife, was ready and willing to lay down her life for Rochalle, if she thought that it would contribute to her welfare. It was always, Rochalle this, and Rochalle that! Whenever she came upon anything in the shape of a dainty—something which was not to be had every day of the week—she was sure to bring it home for Rochalle. And, she went out of her way to procure these dainties as frequently as possible; for, she looked upon Rochalle as one looks upon a child that is delicate and full of strange caprices. The moment Rochalle opened her eyes in the mornings, she found that her mother-in-law had already placed something for her to eat by her bedside, so that she might see it the very moment she opened her eyes. It did not seem to matter to Dvossa-Malka that she had such a great lot of work to do besides all these labours of love which she was always ready to undertake for Rochalle's comfort. Nothing seemed to matter to her but the one thing—that Rochalle should have the very best that money could buy or labour create. Though she had to attend to her business of selling her wares at the market, she felt that the only thing which really concerned her was the care of Rochalle.

"Why should you trouble yourself about me?" asked Rochalle, a hundred times a week.

"What harm is it? You eat this, Rochalle; it is good. And, drink this, Rochalle, it is refreshing." And, Dvossa-Malka kept on fussing around Rochalle day and night. Many times she set the whole house into a commotion by rushing in from the market, breathless, with haste and excitement, to see if Rochalle had got this or that. It was a usual thing for her to pour out a volume of abuse on the unoffending heard of her serving-maid because of her neglect of Rochalle—neglect which was often as imaginary as real. One would think that Dvossa-Malka was trying to run away from a highwayman, from the manner in which she flew into the house sometimes.

"What is it, mother?" Rochalle would ask, fearing that some disaster had befallen her.

"What else should it be but the fool of a girl forgot to take the milk that I left to boil for you off the fire. Oh, may her breath boil within her. I thought she would forget, and so leave you without your hot milk, through letting it burn or boil over. The moment I remembered the milk, I ran off from my stall towards home, as if a mad animal were chasing me. That is how it is. I pay her to do the work, and I a worried to death because she is sure to forget every single thing, unless I am here to keep watch over her. God help me, I don't know where in the world I am at all. I left the shop by itself. And, there stands that ne'er-do-well with his hands folded behind his back, as if there was nothing at all for him to do—as if he were the principal guest at a wedding-feast, and had only to wait for people to attend on him. I asked him to run over with these little cakes for you; but, he would not stir. Here, eat them, Rochalle; they are very good. I got them for you from Leah-Bass, the baker woman. I never buy them from anyone else—not even if I were to be given their weight in gold for nothing. God help Leah-Bass for all that she differs through her drunkard of a husband! How the earth holds such a creature I do not understand. He is a disgrace to every-body, and his poor father must be put to shame in the other world through him. Yes, what was I going to say? My head is confused! Ha, there she goes, the lazy, good-for-nothing girl! Where were you, devil?"

At sight of her, Dvossa-Malka let out a long series of abuses and curses and loud, ear-splitting yells. She cries that Rochalle's breakfast was delayed, the coffee spoiled, and a dozen other misdeeds performed by the girl, all of them bearing more or less on the subject or Rochalle's comfort. In short, the whole house is in a state of irruption through Rochalle. Even Isaac-Naphtali himself, who was always deeply engrossed in his own affairs, often paused to look at Rochalle, and to ask whether she had this or that.

All this anxiety about her, and the constant attendance on the very least of her wants, was highly distasteful to Rochalle. She felt that they only bothered her, and deprived her of her personal freedom to do what she liked, and when she liked, and how. And, over all lay the great truth—that she was not at all as deeply attached to her parents-in-law-as they were to her. She left Moshe-Mendel out of her reckoning, though he was the principal person to her. He was hardly more to her than a mere figure—a name. Between her and him the relations were such that they could be called neither bad nor good. They said little or nothing to one another. A young man of Moshe-Mendel's caliber could not be expected to sit down and talk with his wife in the middle of the say, as if there was nothing more important, or more interesting, for him to occupy himself with. He went here and there, telling stories, watching the business that went on in the market, or else listening to a discourse at the House of Leaning. And, when he came home at night, he could never get a single moment in which to talk to Rochalle without being interrupted. Isaac-Naphtali was sure to pop his head inside of the door to see what "the children" were doing, or else Dvossa-Malka came into the room, bringing something with her for Rochalle. She was sure to have in her hand a plate, or a jug, or a bowl, or a glass. Or, if she had nothing in the way of a dainty to offer Rochalle, she would bring her in a shawl to protect her shoulders from the cold air. And, she was always enthusiastic, always at fever point, for fear that Rochalle should fail to get the very best of everything.

"Here, Rochalle, taste this new kind of preserve that I have invented. I am sure you will like it," was a favourite remark of hers.

"But, I tell you I tasted it a hundred times already."

"Go away, child! You never tasted it before. You never set eyes on the likes of it in your life."

And, Rochalle was compelled to take another spoonful of the preserve that was already grown as distasteful to her as poison.

"Rochalle, my love, you will be famished. Did you ever see anyone eating as you are eating? One would imagine that you were afraid of the spoon. I don't know how you manage to exist at all. If anyone sees you, they will tear the eyes out of my head for starving you to death. They will curse me into the grave for starving my daughter-in-law. You must eat something, even if it is only to satisfy me that you are not starving. Woe is me!"

"Please let me be. I am not hungry. I cannot eat a mouthful. May I never be more hungry in all my life than I am now."

"Well, do me a favour then. Sometimes a daughter-in-law does a favour to a mother-in-law. And, you must remember that I have a mother's heart. Do not pain me by refusing to eat what I have brought you, even if it is only a mouthful."

Rochalle could never manage to get out of eating what Dvossa-Malka insisted she should eat. And, as she took bite after bite, under the watchful eyes of her mother-in-law, she felt that she must choke sooner or later.

This mode of life, that was in itself a kind of bondage, grew intensely wearisome to Rochalle, despite the fact that she knew very well they were her true and faithful friends, and despite, too, the knowledge she had that they were quite ready to carry out the least of her wishes without an instant's hesitation. She felt that if she asked for something which was as far out of their reach as were the stars in the sky they would make every effort, and strain every nerve to get it for her. There was no excuse; and when Rochalle asked for a thing she must have it at once.

But, a human being is not a bull nor a goose that he or she should be satisfied to do nothing but eat. Nobody could possibly enjoy such a life. No one could feel comfortable in the least to have their footsteps dogged to every hour of the day—to have the road dusted for his feet to tread on, so to say—to feel that his footfalls were being counted, and his bites watched. And, Rochalle was heartily sick of having Dvossa-Malka hanging over her when she sat down, and sitting beside her even when she slept. She hated to feel that her whole life was entirely in the hands of others. She saw now that she had completely lost her independence.

She was feeling bitterly the sad position in which she now found herself at the time when the reader made her acquaintance. She was lonely as well as tied down. She had not a single friend to whom she might unburden herself; and, her own parents were far off. Nor could she explain her position to them. They were full sure that she was happy as the day was long. Their letters to her contained nothing but rejoicings at her good fortune. They expressed their heartiest congratulations in detail to her, and sang loud hymns of thanksgiving for the good fortune that the Lord had sent her; and, expressed the deepest feelings of their hearts, which were that she might continue to enjoy her fortune for ever and ever. They often finished up their letters with the words:

"In joy, and with much gratitude on your account, and with happy hearts. Amen! Selah!"

Deep down in her heart, Rochalle carried a grudge against Moshe-Mendel because he kept her at a distance from him. It was as if he wished to show her that he was infinitely superior to her, and, that she was not on any account to imagine herself as his equal. It was not an unusual thing for a young man of his type to hold himself superior to his wife. In fact, all who were like him considered it beneath their dignity to depend on their wives for anything, and certainly never dreamt of consulting them at any time.

But, in his secret heart, and after his own peculiar fashion, Moshe-Mendel was very fond of Rochalle. He was very faithful to her even in thought, and never entertained the least feeling towards her that was not kind as well as honest in every sense of the word.

One day, not long after they were married, Rochalle was unwell and stayed in bed. And, Moshe-Mendel was filled with concern for her. He never left her side of a second. His heart ached to see how pale and ill she looked. Her sighed and thought to himself that he would gladly give up his last drop of blood if by doing so he could save her a single pang of pain.

"It is heartrending," he said to his mother, the tears glittering in his eyes. "We ought to call n the apothecary, or the *Feldsher!* I cannot bear to see her lying there and burning. It is heartrending!"

She was much better the next morning, but, she did not lave her bed. And, Moshe-Mendel refused to leave her for a moment. He felt that he had now a good opportunity to have a long and pleasant chat with his beautiful wide. He had wished for such an opportunity. But, he had always been disturbed by either his father or mother. He felt that Rochalle, too, wished to talk to him quite as much as he wished to talk with her. He drew his chair closer to the bed, so close that her beautiful head was almost in his arms. She turned her blue eyes on him, and waited for him to speak. But, he did not know what to say, and his eyes sought the floor. It was only when she made a movement, as if she wished to turn towards the window, that he looked up. At that moment she looked up at him, and his eyes sought the window. In this way, fencing with glances, so to speak, some little time passed by.

During the whole of the time they had been married, they had no opportunity of talking together by themselves. And, now that the opportunity had arisen, they felt constrained and ill at ease. They did not know what to say to one another, nor how to say it, supposing that they did know.

Rochalle, being a woman, had to leave the initiative in the hands of Moshe-Mendel; whilst he, as a refined and well-bred young man, waited to hear what she might wish to say to him. Meanwhile they were both silent, and only exchanged glances.

"What is it, Moshe-Mendel?"

"What is what?"

"Why do you look at me so?"

"Who looked at you?"

"You looked at me."

"I looked?"

"Who else looked?"

Rochalle turned away from him; and he, taking the ends of his little beard in his hand, and biting them between his teeth for want of some other way of showing his agitation, sat quite still and looked at her for a long, long time. And, as he looked, he sighed, until, attracted by his sighs, Rochalle turned round suddenly, and caught his eyes fixed on her face.

"What is it, Moshe-Mendel?"

"What is what?"

"Why are you sighing?"

"Who is sighing?"

"I am sighing?"

"Who else is sighing?"

And, they both lapsed into silence, once again. Moshe-Mendel drew still closer to Rochalle. He coughed, and was about to say something.

"Listen, Rochalle.... I mean in connection with what you said...."

The door opened suddenly and Dvossa-Malka rushed in, her eyes gleaming with excitement, and her speech rapid and almost incoherent.

"What do you think? I never knew that the turkeys would go to pieces in the dish. But, I want a plate. In the middle of everything I must go and get him some turkey. And, how do you feel now, Rochalle? I am afraid you caught a heavy cold already. I told you not to stay out in the air without a shawl. I sent again to the apothecary. Isaac-Naphtali has gone himself."

"Let me be, mother. It will pass away. I have never been like this before. And, besides, everybody has a cold now. It is going."

"Everything is always all right with you. Go, child, you are talking nonsense. Colds are not going now. Nobody else is laid up. But, I had better sit down a little while." So saying, Dvossa-Malka drew a stool over to the bed and sat down.

"Do you know what, mother?" Moshe-Mendel ventured to remark. "Do you know what? You go to the shop, and I will stay here with Rochalle."

His eyes met Rochalle's eyes, and he was glad. They seemed to say to him:

"You are perfectly right, Moshe-Mendel."

"I don't know what you are saying. What is there for you to do in the shop? There is nothing in it to look after. I wish my enemies to have no more than there is in the shop this day. But, Moshe-Mendel, you must go to your room, and lie down for a while on your father's bed. You have not slept the whole night."

And, in this way did the happy but fettered Rochalle and Moshe-Mendel spend their lives. They wanted for nothing but the moment's liberty that they never could manage to get for themselves. They never got an opportunity to understand one another because of the constant care and kindness of the two old people. But, neither of them ever said a word about it. Neither did they explain their feelings in the matter to one another. Moshe-Mendel did not feel the situation so keenly. He spent his time in reading now and again, and in going to and from his father's shop. He had frequent intercourse with his comrades, and spent many an amusing hour with them.

In a word, he managed to keep himself alive somehow.

But, Rochalle did not live at all. She ate, and drank, and tasted her mother-in-law's preserves a dozen times a day. She never dipped her finger in cold water, and never came in contact with a single soul. It was not seemly that the daughter-in-law of Isaac-Naphtali should hobnob with everybody and anybody. Whilst, on the other hand, anybody who was a somebody would have nothing at all to do with Isaac-Naphtali's daughter-in-law, because the "somebody" would be sure to hold him, or her, self far above Isaac-Naphtali, both in station as in wealth, just as Isaac-Naphtali himself considered himself far above the other householders of Tasapevka.

And, so it came about that Rochalle's days and months dragged on, as if she were a prisoner. It was again eat, and again sleep, again the cup of coffee, and again Dvoska-Malka with her preserves, from week end to weekend.

XII   ROCHALLE SINGS HER LITTLE SONGS

That was how Rochalle lived her life at the period when she first came upon Stempenyu, at the wedding of Chayam-Benzion's daughter.

We left her standing at the door, on the morning after the wedding, gazing dreamily at the scene before her—the market square of Tasapevka—the shops, the booths, and the wagon drawn by oxen, and the peasant boy in the large hat.

That was the life she was leading when, for the first time, she heard the wonderful sounds that came forth from Stempenyu's fiddle.

She was passionately fond of music, and she had always wanted to hear a good musician, and to know him personally, if possible. When she heard anyone playing or singing, she tried to repeat the melody afterwards in her low, sweet voice. Her parents used to say of her that it was a great pity she was born a woman. She had a man's talents in a woman's body. If she were a man she would have set the world on fire.

It seemed that her parents did not understand that Rochalle had within her a certain power—a certain something which we, in our day, call by the name of Talent. But to them, her parents, it seemed that Rochalle's power of picking up a melody, and afterwards repeating it accurately—this power, they thought, lay in her brain, and not in her quick ear. They thought she could do this remarkable thing because she had the cleverness which had, from time immemorial, been the special prerogative of the male sex.

Amongst us Jews, brains play the most important parting the regulation of our lives—much more so than the rest of our capacities, and our limbs and bones and muscles combined—the two hundred forty parts, as well call them.

A good head! A good little head! That is the finest thing among us.

To return to our story:

Rochalle sand until she was about fifteen or sixteen years old, as if she were a little bird to whom the whole universe was as free as the air itself. No matter what she heard, whether it was the Cantor singing in the synagogue, or a simple ballad sung by a wandering minstrel—a beggar, or a song which the people around her were in the habit of singing, or a melody that no one else could play but the orchestras which came into the village when there was a wedding—no matter what it was, Rochalle was sure to sing it soon after, in her low, clear and sweet voice. It was worth while listening to her, and the village looked upon her as a source of amusement. But, the moment she was the affianced wife of Moshe-Mendel, her mother said to her:

"Phew! It is enough, my daughter! You will have to give up singing now. When you are living with your parents in law, how will it look if you suddenly start squealing like a bird? What would the people say to that?"

Rochalle recognized that it was considered unseemly to sing. She took her mother's advice, and never sang any more. Not that she never sang at all. Quite unconsciously, she used to break into song now and again.

It was not her fault if she sometimes forgot what was expected of her. If she sang, it was not because she wished to shame her husband's relatives. When one comes upon the source of a river one may stop it from flowing. But when one does not see—when one does not know whence it comes, one cannot stop it. Not only during the time when she was merely engaged to Moshe-Mendel, but even after she was married to him, it happened many times that she forgot herself completely, and began to sing as of old, just as she used to do when she was a little girl, and cold sing as much as she liked without fear of breaking the code of laws laid down for married women. On one or two occasions she forgot that her mother-in-law was in the room, and that she heard every word she sang:

> "Oh, there, of, there,
> On yonder spot,
> Two little doves are standing.
> They talk and they kiss—
> But what can they have to say?

They kiss and they talk—
But what have they to say?"

"Oh, goodness gracious me! See what I have done!"
cried Rochalle, pulling herself up short, as her eyes fell
on her mother-in-law.

"Well, well, I don't know!" was the other's reassuring
answer. She swung out her arms and thrust her nose forward. "See, Rochalle," she added, "I am afraid the
gooseberries are almost too ripe for the jam. Last year
that happened to me, and I lost half a load of gooseberries."

As for singing before Moshe-Mendel—nothing on
earth would have induced her to do it. She felt that it
would be altogether too extravagant a thing to go and
open her mouth in front of her husband, and to sing into
his eyes. She was sure that such a thing had never been
heard of. It may be that Moshe-Mendel would not have
refused to listen to her. Indeed, he might even have gone
so far as to show is appreciation of her voice. He had
heard her sing an odd note at different times; and he
knew that she had a sweet voice. But, how would it have
looked if he had suddenly taken it into his head to stay
at home and listen to his wife singing little songs? A nice
thing for a respectable man to occupy himself with! It
would mean that he deliberately gave the villagers something to talk about, putting it into their very mouths.

On the few occasions when Rochalle had been
singing in his hearing she had not known that he was
near to her. He had listened to her for a little while, and
then he coughed discreetly, to show her that he had only
arrived on the spot, after which he came boldly forward

into the middle of the room.

A whole year passed by. Rochalle was surrounded by good friends and true; but, in spite of that, she felt very lonely. She was neither happy nor unhappy. Her strongest feelings were of loneliness, despite the goodness and the kindness which met her on all sides.

Often, as she sat over her needlework, she would forget where she was, and would start singing. And, always the song reminded her of home and childhood. Her heart melted within her as the memories crowded fast on top of one another.

> "It flies, and it flies,
> The golden bird,
> Over a thousand seas!
> Oh, carry my greetings,
> Oh, golden bird,
> To my mother so far from me!"

Dvossa-Malka was in the habit of stealing over on tip-toe until she was close enough to Rochalle to hear was she was singing. And, when she took in he meaning of the doggered verse, she would say:

"What is the matter, Rochalle? Are you longing for your old home?"

"Oh, no, no, no! I was just singing a little song to myself! Rochalle made haste to reply. She smiled up to Dvossa-Malka—a wistful, tender smile, as she forced back the tears which were rising to her eyes.

We left Rochalle, on the morning after the wedding, standing at the door, and looking out upon the market-square of the village. She was absorbed in reverie, and forgot her surroundings. But, she was soon brought back to reality by our hero—Stempenyu.

This same Stempenyu, who never lifted his eyes off Rochalle's face, had been quick to see her leaving the table and the room. After waiting a little while, he too, left the room. He came out to the door, and, finding Rochalle in the threshold, he took up his place beside her. He started a conversation with her about the village of Tasapevka, and about her own village, Yehupetz, of which he happened to know every nook and corner—all its beauty spots, and all its highways, and byways. He also spoke at length of the village called Skvirro, having heard that she had spent a short time there, on a visit to a friend. Rochalle listened very attentively to him, but she scarcely said one word to his ten.

"Why is it," asked Stempenyu, "that one never sees you going for a walk, neither on Sabbaths, nor on Holy Days? You are in Tasapevka nearly a whole year—more than a year, and you have never yet taken a walk along the Berdettsever Road. You live so far out of the village itself that I never knew you were here at all. It was only yesterday that I got to know it. When I saw you... I wished to talk with you yesterday; but, I could not. Do you not know what our little Jewish villages are like? The moment two persons are seen talking together, the villagers begin to talk about them.

"But, I beg of you to take a walk next Sabbath afternoon along the Berdettsever Road. You will find the whole town there. You will be sure to go there, won't you? You will surely walk on the Berdettserver Road—eh?"

Rochalle had no time to answer him. For, at this very moment, her mother-in-law, Dvossa-Malka, having missed her from the room, had rushed off in search of her. When she found her standing in the doorway, with Stempenyu beside her, she was filled with surprise. "What does this mean?" she asked herself. And, as if he had divined her question, Stempenyu, who had never been known to lose his presence of mind in a critical moment, and who had never been at a loss for a way out of an embarrassing situation—Stempenyu turned to Dvossa-Malka, and said:

"We were talking about the wedding of the Rebbe's daughter in Skvirro. Your daughter-in-law was a child at the time that I was playing at the Rebbe's wedding. She does not remember a single thing about it."

"Certainly not! How could she remember it!" replied Dvossa-Malka. "But, I remember it quite clearly. I was there with my husband; and, we had to sleep in a field overnight, so crowded was the village with strangers."

"But, you can know nothing of the overcrowding,," said Stempenyu. "I will tell you something more than you know." And, he proceeded to tell her a number of stories of all kinds of descriptions. And, while they were thus occupied, Rochalle slipped away from them and went back to her place at the table, at the right-hand side of the bride.

As we have said already, Stemepenyu could talk. But he had yet another quality. He could talk with old women—gossip with them for hours on end. He could talk the teeth out of their heads, as the saying goes, when necessary. Nor did he need any instructions in the art of keeping them completely under the sway of his eloquence. The world repeats a proverb to the effect that a witch trained into witchcraft is worse than one born with the gift. And, Stempenyu had gone through an excellent school, where he acquired the art of fascination until he was a perfect master in it, as we shall see presently.

"What a cheek he has!" cried Rochalle within herself. "The impudence of him to tell me to be sure to walk next Sabbath afternoon along the Berdettsever Road! What next? The idea of it! Only a musician who plays before the public could have such a cheek." Her heart was hot with anger, as she walked home from the wedding-feast.

The Sabbath came round in due course, and Rochalle's husband, as well as her father-in-law and her mother-in-law, betook himself to his bedroom to sleep for the rest of the afternoon. It had been their habit to do so, for years. And, not only their habit, but the habit of everyone around them—the habit which the Jews of Russian villages had inherited from many lines of ancestors.

Rochalle took her place in the open window. She sat quite still, and hummed to herself one of her little songs, under her breath, as she gazed out dreamily at the street in front of her. She saw, as on all other Sabbath afternoons, the girls of the village promenading up and down. They had gay ribbons in their hair, and wore dresses of all colours—red and blue, yellow and green. They had on shiny boots and tiny gloves. They were all either going to or coming from the Berdettsever Road, where they had an opportunity to show off their pretty dresses, and where they walked up and down in rows, stealing glances at the young men, who were also dressed in bright-coloured, tight fitting clothes, and wore the shiniest of shiny boots. There, along the well-known promenade, the girls would drop their eyes and blush scarlet at the least thing. Their hearts fluttered, as they made love after the fashion peculiar to the village from time immemorial.

Rochalle knew what went on there very well. Why should she not know it? It was not so long since she herself had gone abroad with a group of girls, wearing a bunch of bright-coloured ribbons in her hair. But, now everything was different with her.

Rochalle looked about her. Everyone in the house was fast asleep and snoring loudly. Only she herself seemed to be alive. The other three were to her like

dead persons. She felt as if she were in a house alone
with real corpses. She leant her head on her hands, and
there came back to her memory with a rush, a song she
used to sing when she was a little girl:

> "Alone—alone!
> Lonely as a stone!
> I have no one to talk to;
> But to myself, alone!
> Lonely as a stone!
> I have no one to talk to!"

"Good Sabbath!" cried a voice at her elbow. Rochalle
was startled out of her reverie. She lifted her head, and
saw standing in front of her, on the other side of the open
window, the figure of Stempenyu.

"A good Sabbath to you, I say!" he repeated.

"What is this? How did you come here?" Rochalle
wished to ask him, and leave the window without waiting for an answer. But she said instead:

"A good Sabbath to you, and a good year!"

"You did not take my advice and go for a walk on
Berdettsever Road. I looked for you there, but in vain. I
have... I am... here, read this!"

Stempenyu handed Rochalle a folded sheet of paper,
and vanished.

For a long, long time Rochalle held the paper in her
hand, not knowing what to do with it, and failed to
understand what it was all about. But when the first flush
of excitement was over, she opened the letter and found
that it was written on a large sheet of paper, in plain
Yiddish, and with many errors both of spelling and con-

struction.

"MY DARLING ANGEL FROM HEAVEN," it ran,—"When I saw your heavenly form for the first time my eyes were dazzled, and in my heart a fierce flame of love sprang up. You are my soul—the light of my life. My heart was drawn towards you from the very first. And your beautiful face and you heavenly eyes enraptured me. My soul, my heart and my life are yours. I dream of you, and without you the sun itself is turned to darkness. And I tremble in every limb lest I know not what. I will love you for ever and ever and ever, until my light goes out. I follow your footsteps from afar and kiss the ground you have trodden on, and a thousand times I kiss your beautiful eyes.

STEMPENYU"

Let us now leave the "Queen's Daughter," and turn back to the "King's Son." We will leave Rochalle, and talk only of Stempenyu.

It is true that the letter he had handed to Rochalle was by no means well written. But, that could not be helped. Stempenyu was undoubtedly a hero—a handsome scamp. He could do many things well, but he was not the least bit of a scholar. His father, Berrel Bass—peace be unto him!—had seen that Stempenyu was anxious to play music, and that he refused to learn anything else, though one burned him and baked him alive. He, therefore, gave up all attempts to make of him anything else but a musician. He took him into his orchestra, and put him through all sorts of ordeals in order to test his mettle, with the result that Stempenyu got his own way, and kept his fiddle, from which profession he never had the lest desire to run away.

Berrel Bass had had other children beside
Stempenyu, and they were all musicians. But,
Stempenyu outdistanced them all by a great length. He
seemed to have in him a spark of his grandfather's
genius—his grandfather, Shmulik Trumpet, who had
been personally acquainted with the great Paganini.

In his twelfth year, Stempenyu could already play the
bridal march which was played when the ceremony of
seating the bride was taking place. And, he could play all
the pieces which were necessary for an entire wedding-
feast, including the music of all the dances. For the
exceptional talent which he thus showed the world, his
father, Berrel Bass, loved him more than any of the other
children, who went in rags, half naked and barefooted,
while Stempenyu had good clothes and looked smart and
clean. And, although he often beat him black and blue,
and pulled his ears, and thumped him, and pinched him,
and inflicted on him all sorts of bodily torture, his father
still regarded him as the light of his eyes—the ornament
of his family—the comfort of his declining years, and the
reward for all his labors and trials. He showed off with
him, and pushed him into the eyes of strangers at every
opportunity. He used to say of him, with a proud air, "Do
you see, devils, this youngster will support me in my old
age. It is all right. I can depend on him!"

But, Berrel Bass was not destined to be supported by
Stempenyu in his old age. For, when Stempenyu was
about fifteen years old, he left his father and his home in
search of adventure, with only a few coppers in his pocket, and an old broken fiddle hidden away under his coat-
tails. He wished to see the whole world. And, he wan-

dered in and out of all and made every possible hole and corner, through many towns and villages, in the company of many different orchestras. He would not stay in the same place for more than a six-month at the outside. He always drawn towards some new place—somewhere where he had not been, and which was further and further away from his home. From Tasapevka he went to Stepevka, from Stepevka to Karretz, from Karretz to Balta, from Balta to Old Constantin, and from there to Berdettsev; and so on, always further and further, until at least he found himself in Odessa, from which city he turned back again towards home. On his return journey, he stopped again at every little town and village where he had the least opportunity of being head to any advantage. According to his wishes, so it fell out. He was heard everywhere, and his fame spread like wild-fire. Wherever he went, he found that the people had already heard of him in advance of his coming—had heard that there was a certain musician called Stempenyu, who was going about from place to place, all the world over, playing his fiddle with so much genius that the like of his music had never been heard before since the sawn of creation.

It may be gathered from what was said of him that the greatest excitement prevailed whenever he made his appearance in a community. At eighteen years of age, he had already an orchestra of his own, traveling about, and playing at the most important wedding feasts and other gatherings. And, in this way, in the course of time, Stempenyu gave up playing in other orchestras, as he had to do before; for instance, the Conatopar Orchestra, the fame of which was very great, or the Shmielor, or the

Viennese, or the Sarragrada, or any other of the orchestras which were known everywhere, and for which he had played at different times.

It stands to reason that Stempenyu's success brought him very few friends, and many enemies. As the latter put it, he tore the bread out of the mouths of other musicians. And, on his head were poured out many cart-loads of oaths and curses every day of the week, and every hour of the day. But, to his face he was flattered, and made much of, though the words were born out of malice and spite. Every individual musician knew in his heart that the moment Stempenyu took his fiddle in his hand there was nothing left for any of them to do but to go to bed.

For generations past, the majority of musicians have been passionately attached to the practice of story-telling. They would listen for hours on end to all sorts of tales, of fairies and witches and wonderful doings, legends and romances. And, the members of Stempenyu's orchestra were not exceptional. They not only listened to stories with pleasure, but themselves told many wherever they went. Stempenyu was their hero, and all their stories centered around him. He was, according to the stories, the most marvelous and the most terrible man who had ever lived. And, there arose a belief in the towns and villages to the effect that Stempenyu had sold himself to the Evil One, and that his fiddle had belonged to the great Paganni himself, whose soul still dwelt in it.

When the local musicians heard that Stempenyu and his orchestra were coming into the village, they cursed him and his assistants for hours on end. And, it is hardly necessary to add that their wives took up the cudgels against Stempenyu, and positively poured out on him a terrific flood of such curses as made one tremble to listen to, and lifted the hair of one's head with fear.

The whole year round, the local orchestras were starved, worn thin as laths with the anxiety of borrowing, and pawning, and trying to get this and that on trust. They were so poor that they almost ate up their own skins, since nothing else was available. And to what end? Because they knew that on such and such a date, the daughter of such and such a man of wealth was going to be married. And, they hoped to make a few *roubles* out of the marriage-feast. But, what happened? At the end of their period of waiting, when they were about to tune up their instruments, behold there came into the village an evil spirit—a stranger from goodness alone knew where, and snatched the piece of bread from between the very teeth of the musicians!

"Oh, may the thunder strike down Stempenyu! May the lightning shrivel him up!"

But, from a personal point of view, Stempenyu made no enemies anywhere. He was a good comrade to everybody who had need of him. When he was done with his work of playing at a wedding, he generally gathered together all the musicians of the village, and gave them a grand supper on the most lavish scale possible. He did not economize the liquor, and got the finest dainties that were to be had, without caring a rap for the cost. And, before he left the village, he gave the boys and girls handfuls of coppers, so that they might not forget that he had been amongst them. In a word, he was the best of companions, and the very soul of liberality.

"Do you know what?" the wives of the local musicians said to one another, after Stempenyu had been in their village and had gone away again. "Do you know what? No one ought to attempt to weigh and measure a Jewish heart!"

Above all, Stempenyu found favour in the black or the blue eyes of the daughters of the musicians. Whenever he came, he was sure to seek out the young and pretty girls, and to swear to each and every one of them that he loved her to distraction. And, it was quite true. Stempenyu had the peculiar gift of being able to fall madly in love without a moment's hesitation with the very first pretty girl that came his way. But, no sooner had he crossed the boundary which separated the village she lived in from the next village, than he forgot all about the transports of love into which he had fallen, and never gave a second thought to the girl he had vowed love to for ever. His outbursts of passion as well as his protestations were sure to vanish as the smoke vanishes in the wind. And, the moment he found himself face to face with another pretty girl, in the very next village he came to, he was sure to fall as madly in love with her as he had fallen love with the other girls he had come upon, in the villages he had come away from. He swore that he would never leave her. He protested loudly and emphatically that he would ever forget her as long has he lived. He made her presents, and when the time came for his going away he took leave of her in the most heartrending accents, and was soon on his way to the next village, where he was sure to repeat the same performance of love-making with as much zest as if he had never done it in his life before.

It cannot be said that all his love-affairs ended with his

going away. He was not forgotten by the girls as easily as he forgot them. Generally speaking, the girls to whom he made love took him as lightly as he took them. They attached no importance to his words. They forgot soon after every word he had spoken and every tear he had shed for them. They married, without giving another thought to Stempenyu, the first eligible young man who happened to come in their way. But, on the other hand, it happened in several instances that the girl did not forget Stempenyu, but hoped that he would return to her as soon as he could, to redeem his promise to her. If he did not come back today, then he would surely come on the morrow. If not on the morrow, then on the next day. Until, because of their deferred hopes, they grew heart-sick and weary, and began to pine away. So that at the very moment when Stempenyu was making love to and stealing kisses from a pretty girl in some dark corner, several other girls were pining away for love of him, and were broken hearted because of his absence. They drooped, and languished, and grew thin and fretful, because he had loved them and gone away again without every sending them the least sign that he thought of them any more, much less coming back to claim them for his own. He seemed to have forgotten that they existed, much less that they were waiting for him.

Stempenyu left many heart-broken girls behind him in almost every village he came to with his orchestra. But, he did not always get off scot-free. It happened on one occasion that he could not extricate himself from his entanglement. He had gone a little too far, and was compelled almost by force to marry the girl, despite the fact that he rebelled strongly, and swore that he had never had the least wish to marry her.

Once upon a time, Stempenyu came into the village of Tasapevka and played for three weddings, in partnership with the local orchestra, the members of which had come to him in a body and had taken a terrible oath before him that they would break every bone in his body if he did not agree to divide the proceeds of the wedding with them. Nor would they have spared him if he had not agreed to satisfy their demands at once, which he did, having a kind heart and being utterly opposed to vexing anybody. So they all played together at the weddings, and peace reigned among the musicians.

Between each of the weddings there was an interval of several days, during which Stempenyu had nothing at all to do. He went out amongst the families of the local musicians, and made the acquaintance of Isaiah the Fiddler's daughter—a finely built girl of about twenty-two years old. She had a swarthy complexion, black hair like a raven's wings, and dark eyes that had a green glitter in them. Stempenyu fell madly in love with her, after the fashion that was usual with him. He kissed her, and embraced her, and bought her presents; and, when the time came for him to go away, the young woman, whose name was Freidel, told him to make no mistake. She was not going to let him go until he had affianced himself to her, openly and publicly, according to the customs which obtained in the village. She was going to bind him to her as effectually as was possible. Stempenyu was not used to engaging himself publicly to any of the girls he made love to, and he tried to drag himself free from the net into which he had entangled himself. He twisted and turned, and argued at great length, and pulled this way and that; but, all to no purpose. Freidel was a girl with a strong will. She had made up her mind to keep Stempenyu by her side forever, now that she had him in her clutches, and would not dream of letting him escape from her. He was compelled to do as she wished. The formal engagement took place amidst great rejoicing. All the musicians of the village came together, and by their united forces, succeeded in making a grand spree in honour of the famous bridegroom. And, in the house of Isaiah the Fiddler, the rejoicings were kept up for three days on end.

At last Stempenyu managed in getting free of the people, and he left the village to go on his rounds to the other places, where he was waited for.

Naturally, he set out to forget his engagement as soon as possible—to shake himself free, metaphorically speaking, of Freidel and everybody and everything connected with her. And, he conducted himself quite as usual. That is to say, he flirted desperately in every village he came to, according to his old habit. He had a good time, wherever he found himself with his orchestra, and thought of nothing, when suddenly....

There is no such thing in the world as everlasting happiness. Everything changes sooner or later. Everything is only for a certain time. And, Stempenyu's freedom was destined to be snatched from him for ever. And evil destiny had set out in pursuit of him. An evil spirit laid hands on him, and in a moment overthrew his careless, joyous youth forever. A great misfortune befell him.

He was playing at a wedding in a little town somewhere in Malo-Russia, and was carrying on a love affair with a pretty girl of the village, the only daughter of Hirshka the Flautist, and was one day in the middle of making all sorts of promises to her to come back and marry her, when Michsa the Drummer with sleepy face came over to him, gave him a dig in the ribs, regardless of the presence of the village girl, winked at him and said to him, in a whisper which did not reach her:

"Go, Stempenyu, there in the house a girl is waiting for you."

"A girl? What sort of girl?"

"A dark girl with green eyes."

Stempenyu went over to the house, and found that the girl who was waiting for him was no other than his affianced wife, Freidel, the daughter of Isaiah the Fiddler Tasapevka.

"Why do you look so hard at me, Stempenyu? Do you not know me? Ha! ha! How he squints and blinks his eyes at me. It is I, Stempenyu. Freidel, your own Freidel, Isaiah the Fiddler's daughter."

"Well, I know that. And what then? I don't know you? Of course I do. But how did you get here? And what have you come for?"

"How did I get here? With my feet, Stempenyu—with my feet, I tell you. I asked my way at every step, until I came at last to the house of Hirksha the Flautist. And, where do I come from? From home, of course. How else could it be?"

"Well, and what news is there at home? When did you leave?"

"What news can there be, Stempenyu? There is no news. When did I leave home? I left home about six or seven weeks ago. We were everywhere you like. Wherever we came, we were told that you had been there, but had gone away again, until at last we arrived at the right place. Well, and how are you, Stempenyu? Are you well?"

"What? I? How should it be with me? Come, Freidel. Why are we standing here?" he added, seeing that a group of musicians had gathered around him, and were staring at him with curiosity as well as the dark girl with the black hair who had just come into the village.

"For my part, let us go," she answered.

Stempenyu snatched up his overcoat and his walking stick, and went out into the village by the side of Friedel the Black-One. He looked around to see that no one was within hearing distance, and he addressed her in a firm voice:

"Tell me, I pray you, what this means?"

"What do you mean by asking what this means?"

"I mean—why have you come here?"

"Listen to him!" she exclaimed. "One would imagine he was dead as a door-nail, or goodness knows only what!"

"Do you hear, Freidel?" Stempenyu demanded. "Do you hear me, Freidel? I don't like to have such tricks played on me. I asked you plainly what you are doing here, and you answered me with ridicule. I want none of that."

Freidel threw a sharp glance at him out of the corners of her green eyes, swept back the long plait which had fallen forward over her shoulder, and answered him in a serious voice:

"You want to know what I am doing here? I came to see you Stempenyu. On the day of our betrothal, you said you would write to me the moment you set foot in the village for which you were bound. You promised that you would make arrangements immediately for our wedding to take place in two or three weeks' time. I waited and waited to hear from you for more than two months, but, you wrote never so much as a word. So, we decided to go out into the world in search of you. And, we found that looking for you was like looking for the day before yesterday. We were in every corner of the world, and now at last the Lord took pity on us, and we—"

"Tell me, Freidel, who are 'we'? You said 'we' each time. 'We' went and 'we' came."

"We two. That is my mother and I, Stempenyu."

"Your mother!" cried Stempenyu. And, all at once he felt that he was a beaten man. "Your mother? What is she doing here?"

"Hush! What are you shouting for, Stempenyu? What

did you suppose? No girl travels by herself. It would be a nice thing to do, eh?"

"True. But, what business has your mother with me?" asked Stempenyu, as he turned round, and retraced his steps back to the village.

"She is my mother, and will become your mother-in-law. You must remember that, Stempenyu."

"And, do you really imagine, Freidel, that I am going to marry you?"

"Well, and what do you think yourself, Stempenyu?"

"Nonsense!"

"Why is it nonsense?"

"Because I never thought seriously of marrying you at all."

Freidel stopped, and gazed at Stempenyu, right into his eyes. Then she looked about her on all sides to see if there was anyone near them. She drew closer to Stempenyu, and whispered to him hurriedly:

"Listen to me, Stempenyu. Don't imagine that you have to do with a timid little girl who does not know anything of what foes on in the world. I know you well, Stempenyu. I know that you are a thorough-going charlatan. You would like to have a different girl to flirt with every day of the week. But, all this does not matter now. Everything has to come to an end at some time or another. Isn't it so? In reality, you are not a bad sort, by any means. It is all because your heart is so soft. But, you are handsome, too—a man in ten thousand. And, your playing is marvelous. You can always provide for a wife. And, for these reasons, I want you. You must marry me, and that speedily. And, all your protests are in vain—a mere waste of breath. Bend your head a little lower, and I will tell you a secret."

Freidel's secret sent a thrill through Stempenyu's frame. He was unable to lift a hand or a foot. He was like turned to stone. He remained standing stock still in the middle of the road, and could not even open his mouth to utter a single word. At this juncture there arrived upon the scene, panting and breathless, the red haired Michsa Drummer. He was looking for Stempenyu to tell him that the wealthiest man of the village was waiting for him to make arrangements to have him play at his daughter's wedding.

Stempenyu pared from Freidel with a sigh. His last words were:

"We will meet again, Freidel."

"There is no doubt that we will meet again," was Freidel's reply. And, she parted from Stempenyu well satisfied with the progress of affairs.

Everyone who saw Stempenyu when he played at that wedding was surprised at the pallor of his countenance, and the abstracted, glassy stare that was in his eyes. He looked far worse than many a man who was about to be laid in his grave. His carelessness and his joviality had been taken from him as with a hand. And, within himself, Stempenyu was feeling that the end of his old free life had come. He would never again be able to fly here and there like a bird of the high heavens. He was about to take upon his shoulders an everlasting yoke. Farewell to moonlight walks with pretty girls! Farewell to laughing eyes and ruddy lips! Farewell to silver, starlit nights of enchantment!

It was true that Stempenyu did not give in to his bondage without a struggle. But, he was as a fish that is caught in a net, and, no amount of struggling was of the least avail.

Freidel and her mother were arrayed in battle against him, and he could not hope to fight them down. Indeed, he was afraid to say a word. Especially was he afraid of Freidel's mother. She was in the habit of screwing up her tiny black face until it almost disappeared from sight, and only her black eyes were to be seen burning in her head like two living coals. She looked so vicious that Stempenyu was afraid she would pounce down upon him, and tear him to pieces as a wild cat tears its prey, scratching the eyes out of his head, and clawing him all over. He felt that she kept herself from falling upon him only because Freidel held her back from doing so. He knew that she would not permit it. He was as sure of it as if he had actually heard her say:

"Do not interfere, mother. You will only make things worse. You had better do nothing and say nothing. Just look on in silence. But, be sure to keep a strict watch over him at every step he takes. He is a slippery customer, and may succeed in tearing himself free from our grip, in spite of all our precautions. But, and all will be well, mother, all will be well. Stempenyu is mine—he is mine!"

Freidel had held out stubbornly, and in the end succeeded in getting what she wanted. She married Stempenyu
according to all the laws and customs which were the
most binding—that might serve to tighten the grip she
had on him already. And, very soon after the wedding-
day, she took him in hand, and began to tyrannize over
him to her heart's content, aided considerably by her
mother, who could hardly contain herself in patience till
the great day came round at last when she was the mother of a married daughter.

And, Stempenyu tasted the bitterness of hell, and got
to know the taste of it thoroughly. He was now wide
awake to the minutest thing that concerned him, and
soon got to know every separate shade of difference
which existed between his old free life and his new life,
that was one long bondage.

After they were married, the young couple went and settled in the village of Tasapevka, to which she belonged. He and his company made the village their permanent headquarters.

There was no more going about for Stempenyu, no more wandering joyously and carelessly over the face of the earth. Freidel took care to impress upon him the fact that she was altogether opposed to his wandering life. He was her slave now, and he had to obey her slightest wish, though it was true that she managed him only through kindness, and by means of gentle persuasion.

And, there began for Stemepenyu a new life—a brand new life, as one might say. Before his marriage, he had been a mad of great pride and independence of spirit; but, no sooner had he become Freidel's husband than he lost both his pride and his independence. All his strength was gone from him as well as his good-humour, and his sparkle of wit. In his own house, Stempenyu had no authority whatever.

"Keep in mind only what concerns you," was Freidel's argument. "Your business is with the orchestra and with the music, and with weddings and other parties where you are asked to play. What do you want money for, you little fool?"

After this fashion did Freidel succeed in extracting from him every single *kopek* he ever earned anywhere.

She was very fond of money. She had been brought up in extreme poverty, and had had very few opportunities of handling even the smallest sum of money. As a girl she had found it extremely difficult to procure of a piece of ribbon for her hair, or a comb, such as all the other girls wore. She never got anything she wanted before she had shed a little flood of tears of the bitterest and most despairing kind. Until she was fifteen years old, she went about barefooted and almost in rags. Her mother had gone out as a nurse to other families, talking care of tiny children. And, Freidel got many beatings from her mother and father, Isaiah the Fiddler, who had a decided weakness for strong drink. Though she had never enough to eat, Freidel was early filled with a passion for money. Her greed knew no bounds, and was only aggravated because of her wretched poverty. It was only at the Feast of the *Purim*, when she earned a few coppers on her own account, that she had an opportunity of holding some coins in her hand for a length of time. These coppers were given to her by the people for whom she carried out the customary *Purim* gifts to friends, from one end of the village to another. She used to hide her coppers in the bosom of her bodice so that her mother might have no chance of dragging them out of her on any pretense whatever. At night, she slept with the coins under her pillow, and in the day, she clutched them to her greedily. And, when the Festival of *Pesach* came round at last, Freidel rushed off to the fair to buy with her money the ribbons and other ornaments of personal adornment that she had long wished for and dreamt of in her wildest dreams.

No one took the least notice of Freidel until she was about eighteen years old, when she suddenly sprang up, as a gourd in the night, from a little girl to a tall, dark, heavily-built young woman of mature physique.

When she became engaged to Stempenyu, she herself did not realize the good fortune which had befallen her. But, her mother saw everything with her lynx eyes.

A hundred times a day, she explained to Freidel that Stempenyu was a treasure—a little gold-mine in himself, even thought he was a charlatan and a good-for-nothing as well, into the bargain, so to speak. He was a man to whom the *roubles* were of no value; and, hence, she must make it her business to manage him in all things as she herself had always managed her husband, Freidel's father, Isaiah the Fiddler.

After Freidel had married Stempenyu, she remembered and applied every word of advice which her mother had given her—had drilled into her, rather. Gradually and completely, she took all the authority out of Stempenyu's hands. She proved to him times out of number that a woman must know everything connected with her husband, that a man's wife was not a stranger to him, and that a daughter of the Jewish people was not the kind of woman who created for herself different interests from those which concerned her husband. No, she was at one with him in everything. He must know that. He must realize clearly, once and for all, that he was she, and she was he. In short, he must not fail to see that he had a wife who was only his second self.

When Freidel became the mistress of the house, she saw that Stempenyu was always making more and more money. He often brought home a handful of silver *roubles*. She threw herself upon them with the greed of a hungry person before whom has been set a tasty dish, and an appetizing one. But, the money itself brought her neither pleasure nor satisfaction. She was continually harassed by the fear that there might be no more on the morrow. Perhaps her husband might one day be incapacitated from ever earning another *kopek* again! So she tied up the money in many knots and not only that, but she began to scrape together one *kopek* on top of the other with a sort of feverish anxiety.

"Why are you always complaining and protesting that we can't afford this and that?" asked Stempenyu, whenever he heard her talk of the terrible possibilities which stood before her eyes like ghosts, haunting her by day as well as by night. And, she answered him evasively:

"If you knew everything you would grow old before your time. Never mind, Stempenyu," she added, with a smile. But, she went on doing as she thought it was her duty to do—saving, and stinting, and economizing in a thousand different ways. On all sides she kept reducing her household expenses. She bought in as little as possible, kept a badly filled larder, and cut down the number and variety of the day's meals to a minimum. She herself often refrained from eating and drinking, so that she might add another few coins to her hoard at the end of a few days. Presently, she began to do business with the money she had saved. She lent it out on securities of different kinds, and so succeeded in earning a percentage on the money which, otherwise, might have brought her no profit. She began the business by lending a few *roubles* to a neighbor in a friendly way. Why not? she asked herself. And, as time went on, she saw that capital was not touched; but that, on the contrary, one *rouble* soon grew into two, almost without the least bother. It was not long before she had entered heart and soul into the business of lending money as a regular means of making money. And, as her business grew, her rapacity, her usury grew also. She developed all the cunning and all the meanness which have from time immemorial been connected with money-lending. She was like so many of our wealthy folks who follow the same calling, and are not ashamed of it.

It was remarkable that Freidel should have within her such a terrible love of money. She could not have inherited the passion from her father, Isaiah the Fiddler. Neither could she have acquired this feeling by imitating her father's friends, the other musicians, for amongst them there was not one who cared very much about the *roubles*, or who kept a tight hold on the *kopeks*. A Jewish musician, at that period, was something like a nigger, a wandering gipsy rather. He belonged to a distinct and separate species of mankind. He had even a jargon of his own which no one else understood; and, he had his own peculiar manners, and customs, and traditions.

He was always jolly and in the height of good humor. He danced and sang and played all sorts of games to amuse himself. Her always talked of lively things, and seemed to care nothing if he turned the whole world upside down. When he came home to his wife and children he made merry, and lived on cakes and sweets if he had the money. Or if he hadn't, he starved with the same cheerfulness. But, he never cared about the morrow. Neither did he seem to care whether he had the money he needed or not. Life itself was enough for him, and he wanted but little to induce him to dance and sing and make merry, even if had to go without meals for days. After a supperless night, he went a-borrowing without a moment's thought; or else he pawned the very pillows he had to sleep on. And, when he did get them back, he knew that it would not be long before he would pawn them all over again as before. And, the children of the musicians were also jolly. They were easy-going, devil-may-care the sort of creatures, the daughters as well as the sons. Their lives, no more than their faces, were not covered over in with veils of worry or anxiety. In a word, the life of a musician had all the qualities as well as all the drawbacks of those who dwell in earthly paradise. And, living in this way, how could he ever occupy himself with fretting about the future? How could he possibly leave off his play to fret himself about the morrow?

Freidel's father, Isaiah, was not a weeping soul. He was, in nature, utterly unlike other poor men. He did not interest himself in his poverty. On the contrary, he was always lively and gay. No sooner did he earn a *rouble* did he spend it in the same breath, as one might say. And, Freidel's mother was also found of good things. That is to say, of good living—good eating and drinking. She would have dainties, even if she had to pawn her pillows to procure them. And, in order to prove that her love of dainties was only right and normal, she was ready to quote a number of proverbs all of them bearing on the same thing, that it was apparent to the wisest as well as the most foolish of mankind that all a man's work was only for his stomach, and that it was better to spend one's money on the baker than on the doctor. And, after all, what was a man's life that he should deny himself what his heart desired?

Even amongst the extravagant musicians and their extravagant wives, Freidel's mother was considered the most extravagant.

And, how did Freidel manage to have such a stingy soul? Where did she get her miserliness? Perhaps the quality came to her through having spent her life in such abject poverty that she never had a *groschen* of her own, and through having suffered so keenly and so frequently the pangs of hunger, in the days of her childhood, when she was most open to receive strong and permanent impressions.

Or, it may have been that the soul of a mises who had died long ago, happened to lose its way, and to wander into the body of the young girl, where it found a resting place for itself. However that may have been, the fact remained that Freidel moaned and wailed at the very mention of the word money. And, the time soon came when her wealth was the envy of all the musicians of the village. They could not help remarking on her exceedingly good fortune, every time they thought of her.

Only in one thing was Freidel unlucky—she had no children. And, who can tell if that was not the very reason why she gave herself up, heart and soul, to the business of making money? The keenest enjoyment that one gets out of life—the enjoyment that one gets out of watching and tending one's own children—was denied to her. And, hence, it is likely that she turned her feelings in an altogether different direction. As a rule we find that the women who have no children are crankiest of all. They seem to be lacking in the goodness and gentleness of other women. They can have no love left in them for anyone but themselves.

Freidel was just such a woman. Only, it could not be said of her that she disliked Stempenyu. Why should she not love him after all? Was he not the handsomest man in the village—a perfect picture? And, was he not the best player of a thousand players? And—this was the main thing—could he not earn plenty of money? Was he not a gold-spinner, as her mother had said? "My Stempenyu," Freidel would say, in a boasting tone of voice, to her women friends, "my Stempenyu has only to draw the bow across his fiddle once and he has made a *rouble*—two draws means two *roubles*—three draws means three *roubles*. Do you follow me?"

But, to Stempenyu himself, the *rouble* had no value. He played at a wedding, and got his pockets filled with money, and cared not a rap about it. When he had it, he gave it away liberally, or pretended to lend it to a comrade forever. In the same way, if he was short, he went borrowing from other folks. He was a real artist, full of the temper and tone of the man who cares nothing about the whole world—whose life begins and ends with art. He cared only about his music—about keeping up his orchestra. His mind was centred on new overtures and new operatic pieces. He arranged a wedding, and played for it to the very best of his ability, not pell-mell—anyhow. He listened attentively to the promptings of his artistic conscience.

There were two things which Stempenyu loved best in the world. First himself, and next his fiddle. He had a lot to do to take care of himself as he wished to. He dressed well and in the latest fashion, waxed his moustache and kept his hair in curl. In short, he was a good deal of a dandy in his own way. And, when he was thinking of himself, he invariably forgot his fiddle. But, contrawise, when he had his fiddle in his hand, he forgot not only himself but the whole world. When he was filled with sad thoughts, or overcome with melancholy, he took up his fiddle, licked the door of his room, and played and played for hours on end. He composed the most fantastic pieces, and improvised all sorts of curious combinations. He played whatever came first into his head, regardless of everything. And, he poured out his soul in the most mournful cadences that grew sadder and softer each minute.

Suddenly, he would be seized with a wild fit of temper, and he would play the most bizarre things, his tones growing louder and more stormy each moment, just as they had grown softer only a little while before. So extreme was his violence that it was not long before he was exhausted. He sighed several times in succession, and the self pity welled up in his heart in great gushes.

By and by, his anger died away. His wrath was stilled, and, once again, he poured out his heart in a series of low, solemn, yet sentimental sounds. And it was not long before his good humor was restored, and, he was as lively and as merry as he had been before—as was habitual with him.

It did not happen often that he betook himself to his room in order to play off his melancholy mood. As a rule, he was not easily put out; but, when it did happen that he had been angered or saddened, it took him quite a long while before he was restored to his normal mood. He found it impossible to tear himself away from his fiddle once he had taken it in hand, and he played until he was quite tired out, and could play no more. His imagination once enkindled, he was like a mighty torrent of the wilderness. He only grew in strength as the minutes flew by. He cared nothing at all for impediments. His soul melted within him. His feelings ran riot. His talents were at their highest when the flood gates were lifted, and he felt neither compunction nor constraint. His playing was beyond compare when he was in this riotous mood to which one can give no name. And, it seemed to him that he himself was sending up to the throne of the almighty a devoutly-breathed prayer for mercy, from the very bottom of his heart—a prayer which must find its way and gain for him that which he asked for out of his bitterness of soul—mercy.

It is said that the Psalmist had a special orchestra which he set playing while he was composing the psalms in praise of the Lord! Probably this is only a legend; but, it is, nevertheless, a pious imagination of a pious heart.

"Keila the Fat One—may she suffer all my woes—as brought me only one week's interest on the money I lent her. She says she will pay be this week's in a few days."

With a speech of this nature was Freidel wont to greet Stempenyu, as he came forth from his room, after having had his fill of music, his black eyes flaming like two living coals, and his nerves strung to their highest pitch.

His fine blazing eyes had in them a great power of attracting to him every individual on whom he happened to flash them; but no sooner did he catch sight of Freidel than their power went out like candles in the wind. It was as if her presence jarred on him.

The moment Stempenyu came home from a wedding at which he had been playing, Freidel was sure to come forward and meet him with a cunning little smile and with all the playfulness of a kitten—the playfulness that is so beguiling and so disarming. But, she soon explained the reason of her cunning. She wanted to get from him the money he had earned.

"What do you want money for, Stempenyu?" she

would ask, as she emptied his pockets. "What do you want money for? What do you stand in need of? Have you not everything? You are not hungry—far be it from such a thing! And, you are well and fashionably clad. And, when you want a little money sometimes do I not give it to you? Then, let me hold your money for you. I will not spend a single *kopek* on you. Well, give it to me—give it to me!"

Stempenyu stood before her like a child that had just been punished, and Freidel did as she liked with him. He was altogether in the power of Black Freidel.

Ah, what happened to you, Stempenyu, to let yourself fall into the clutches of a mere nobody like Freidel? She dances on your head. And, you are compelled to submit when she leads you by the nose, exactly as Samson the Strong of long ago had to allow himself to be led by his Delilah after she had shorn his locks—after she had beguiled him into laying his head in her lap, thus falling into her power through his momentary weakness.

Phew! it is a shameful thing that has befallen you, Stempenyu!

A pity of Stempenyu!

But, it was not altogether as one imagines. He hardly needed to be pitied. For, though he had no authority in his own home, and was entirely led by a mean woman, he still lived in a world of his own creating—altogether his own, in which Freidel never entered at all. In his own world he was as a prince; and, when he found himself safely within its imaginary walls, he was satisfied, as we shall see presently.

First of all, he spent half of the day practicing his new pieces with his orchestra, along with the members of whom he played an odd prank now and then. He listened gladly to the witty sayings of the jester in the group, and laughed heartily at Michsa Drummer, against whom the jester leveled the most of his shafts. And, often Stempenyu told stories himself, recounting the various adventures he had at this wedding and that. He told how, on one occasion, the bridegroom had stubbornly refused to go under the canopy, would on no account consent to be married until he had got every *kopek* of the dowry that had been promised him counted out into his hand. At another wedding, the bride had fainted away stone dead without cause, and could not be revived for the ceremony to go on until long after the appointed time. Here the jester interrupted Stempenyu to put in a remark apropos of the story. At a third wedding something very funny happened. After supper, when the guests were about to begin dancing for the night, there was a sudden outburst of laughter. No sooner had Stempenyu touched on the incident than all the musicians burst out into a loud guffaw at the memory of what had taken place. It was as if a bomb of laughter had exploded in the middle of the room.

"What are you laughing at?" asked Freidel, from another room. "One would imagine that someone was tickling you."

"Never you mind," was Stempenyu's prompt reply. "I told you hundreds of times not to interfere in our affairs."

And, for one moment, Stempenyu appeared to be the real master of the house—a little Sultan, almost.

When Stempenyu was not practicing or playing by himself, he was occupied with his personal appearance, of which he was very proud. His coats were perfect in cut and colour, and his boots were of the finest leather, and were lacquered until they shone like mirrors. His hair was curled with the utmost precision, every lock separately and every curl in its appointed place. His shirt col-

lars were always white as snow, and he carried in his hand
a stick with a carved ivory handle. And, on his head, he
worse a broad black cloth cap with a shiny peak that
came down almost to his eyes. His head thrown back
proudly, and his body perfectly poised, Stempenyu
walked through the streets with the dignified gait of a
man of the utmost importance—a general, or a governor
of a province. He had many acquaintances everywhere,
all of whom he saluted gracefully and cordially as he
came towards them. When he passed the shops he greeted the young women—the shopkeepers—with much
warmth. The women grew red. They remembered how,
when they were girls, they had known Stempenyu intimately. Those were good times. But now? Who cared
what to-day was like when the memory of yesterday
filled the mind?

There were several young women, and girls too, who
came out to the doors of their shops to talk to
Stempenyu. And, he was delighted to stand and chat
with them about this person and that, and to laugh and
make merry with them. But these chance encounters did
not always pass off without comment. Sometime the
neighbors talked about them, and carried the news of
Stempenyu's little escapades from one house to the
other; and, as they went from house to house, the stories
grew in dimensions, after the fashion that belongs to all
villages where the people have nothing else to interest
themselves with but the most trivial sayings and doings
of their neighbors.

"What are the people talking about you again for? Is
there another story, Stempenyu?"

"What sort of story, Freidel?

"The stories of your own making, I suppose. He asks me! Wherever two people meet you are sure to make a third in a few minutes. The whole village is talking about you again."

"I don't know what you want of me, Freidel?"

"What I want of you? I want you to have done with your old ways. It is time for you. Wherever there is a young woman or a girl to be found in the village, you are sure to know her, and to stand talking to her for three hours by the clock. You can't possibly say enough to her!"

"Ah, I suppose you are referring to the chat I had with Esther, Abraham-Jacob's daughter?"

"Well, if I am referring to Esther, what then? Is she a nun, or what?"

"I had a little business to talk about with her."

"Your business! I know you, Stempenyu."

"And, you may know me! Abraham-Jacob is thinking of making his daughter's wedding in Yehupetz. He took the mad idea into his head. And, when I saw Esther, I talked to her about it. Perhaps I ought not to have talked to her about it? Perhaps I ought to let such a fine wedding go out of our village?"

"What made him think of Yehupetz—the madman?" asked Freidel. And, in her green eyes there was a peculiar glitter which always came into them at the very allusion to money, as well as at the mention of the word.

"There's no use in asking questions about the actions of a lunatic," replied Stempenyu, feeling that he had come out of this scrape without a scar.

He often managed to get out of scrapes. He was very alert, and knew exactly how to deal with Freidel.

Once he had crossed the boundary which separated his village from its neighbors, Stempenyu felt he was once again as free as the air. He could do whatever he wished, without having to give an account of himself. So that, once he found himself in a strange village, he was reluctant to leave it again. And, he had all sorts of adventures wherever he went, both comic and tragic. And, he felt that he was in an altogether different world into which Freidel could not enter. Though she frequently tried to bribe Michsa Drummer to tell her of Stempenyu's doings, she had failed, for Michsa was loyal to his master, and moreover hated Freidel like poison.

And, no sooner did Stempenyu find himself in a new village, than he threw off all traces of his old self. He was an altogether freer and brighter Stempenyu than he had been in his own house—in Freidel's presence.

In the secret world which Stempenyu spent such a large portion of his time, Rochalle began to play an important part—the greatest part that anyone had ever played in his life hitherto. The letter he wrote her, which we have already seen, was full of sincerity and truth. For, he had fallen madly in love with Rochalle the very moment he had set eyes on her at the wedding of Chayam-Benzion's daughter. He did not write the letter at once. It took several days before the fire which Rochalle's blue eyes had enkindled in his heart had burst into flame. And, when he could control his feelings no longer, he locked himself up in his little room, in which he played his fiddle when he was in the mood, and with the same pen, and on the same music-sheets that he used for his compositions, he wrote his letter to Rochalle.

To Stempenyu writing was by no means an easy matter. On the contrary, he found it very difficult, and sweated and toiled before he succeeded in saying what he wished to say. He had never been taught to write, but had himself picked up the rudiments at random, and in a haphazard fashion. And, he felt quite tired and dull after writing only a few lines.

He carried the letter about with him for several days before he found a way of putting it into her hands. Michsa Drummer was a good messenger to send with such letters. But, that was only when they were in strange places. Here it was too risky to employ him; for, since Freidel's eyes penetrated through everything, even Michsa was far from safe. He was decidedly dangerous in such a case. Stempenyu hardly managed to live over the hours until the Sabbath came around. And, the afternoon of that day found him dressing with more than usual care and exactitude. He wore a high hat, in accordance with the very latest fashion of the day. He went out and walked slowly along the Berdettsever Road, hoping that Rochalle would be walking there, too. But, he sought her in vain. All the women and girls of the village were there, promenading up and down, throwing shy glances at Stempenyu, and smiling at him—everybody was there except Rochalle. The letter that was in his pocket would not let him rest. It drew him to her, closer, and still closer every minute.

"Perhaps I ought to go down the street in which Isaac-Naphtali lives. I may see her there," thought Stempenyu. And, he walked along slowly until he came to the open window, behind which Rochalle was sitting, absorbed in a brown study, and singing softly to herself the well-known little song which she used tossing long ago, when she found joy in singing, and was not yet aware of the awfulness of doing what she liked in that matter.

> "Alone—alone!
> Lonely as a stone!
> I have no one to talk to;
> But, to myself alone!
> Lonely as a stone!
> I have no one to talk to!"

When Rochalle heard Stempenyu's "Good Sabbath!" and saw him standing before her, she thought that she was dreaming; for, she had already grown accustomed to seeing Stempenyu in her dreams. But, when she found the music-sheet in her hand, she saw that he had really been and gone again. She read the letter through, got up from her seat, glanced furtively through the window, and said to herself: "It's well for him that he has run away. I would have told him what is what. There's an idea for you! Stempenyu, all of a sudden!"

She caught up the letter, and was about to throw it out the window; but, she checked herself in the nick of time. She read it carefully a second time, folded it and put it in her pocket.

Her anger increased each moment. She would have liked to see Stempenyu, and to ask him face to face what he meant by such conduct, and what name one might give to it. It was the height of impudence to write such a letter. Who was she, and who was he, that he might treat her so shamelessly?

She began to make plans to meet him, preferably in

some quiet place where no one would see them—where she might talk to him, without interruption or fear, and tell him in full what she thought of him. And, a most ingenious plan came into her mind!

"Listen, aunt," said Rochalle to her mother-in-law the morning after she had received Stempenyu's letter. She called Dvossa-Malka "aunt" on special occasions. "If they were not too dear I should like to get a string of corals—good, heavy corals."

"Well, I told you many times to go over to Freidel Stempenyu, and see what she has got. Pick out whatever you like. If you wish, I will go with you. She will give me the corals cheaper than you."

Black Freidel, who now occupied herself regularly with money-lending, and with taking all sorts of goods in pawn, principally jewelry, had ceased to regard her dealings as a mere side-issue. She now looked upon her business as the first interest in her life. She also took to buying and selling the thins which were brought to her as pledges. She gradually refused to do anything for the poor but buy their goods, and so compelled them to give her everything for next to nothing. And, along with this, she bought and sold in the ordinary way also, dealing with the people in the villages around Tasapevka as well as with her immediate neighbors. And, everyone knew that a good string of corals, or anything else that was costly, could be bought of her—of Freidel, the wife of the famous musician Stempenyu.

It was remarkable how clever Freidel was in this business. She understood the value of a thing at first glance, and could talk anyone into buying not what they wished to buy but what she wished to sell them.

When Dvossa-Malka and Rochalle came into her house, she greeted them with a smile. "And, how are you, Dvossa-Malka? You know that I have been wanting to see you this long while back?"

"What for, Freidel?"

"What for, you ask. It's more than a year since your son brought home the beautiful creature that is his wife. And—nothing! You never once brought her to me to let her pick out something suitable to a woman of her great beauty, Ah, Dvossa-Malka, I am ashamed of you."

"You are quite right, Freidel. But, am I to blame if my daughter-in-law does not want a string of corals, or anything else?"

"That's news for you! What do you mean by saying she doesn't want corals! To you it may be all right; but, to me it is all wrong. I would soon persuade her into wanting them!"

And, Freidel proceeded to open a large chest, painted green, from which she drew forth one row of corals after the other, making profuse apologies, and explaining everything in detail, and at great length. And, as she held up for inspection the various ornaments, she kept up a running comment on the many blessings that she wished to fall upon her if they were as she said of them, and of the many curses which were bound to come upon her, if she was exaggerating. She was exactly like all the other business women of the district.

"Do you see, Dvossa-Malka, if you took my advice you would tell your daughter-in-law to take this particular string of corals. May I be as free from evil, and you too, if you can get better corals than these anywhere— real Oriental corals. Excuse me, Rochalle, but I should like to put them around your neck. May I have as good a year as they are just the thing for you. They are the exact thing for your white throat. Wear them in good health; and next year, I hope and trust that your mother-in-law will be able to afford to buy you a set of five rows of such corals—each coral twice the size of those that are now around your neck! Ah, how well they match the pink of your cheeks!"

"Say yourself," she added, turning again to Dvossa-Malka; "say yourself, you who are as good a judge of corals as anyone I ever came across, are not these perfect? I can only wish to have as perfect a year, as beautiful a year, if it pleases the Lord to grant it me!"

When she finished speaking, Freidel took a little mirror out of the chest and held it up so that Rochalle might see herself and the corals. And, Freidel's green eyes glittered with the success of her efforts. But, at the same time, she was bathed in sweat through having to talk so much, and at such great length, and more especially because she had to swear so many round oaths.

"And, your Stempenyu goes on his with work?" Dvossa-Malka, pointing her finger at the door of his room, from which came forth a series of sweet sounds.

"Yes, he is playing in there," replied Freidel, as she went on showing them other strings of corals. And, between her and Dvossa-Malka there ensued a heated argument, such as is usual between women when they start talking of trade.

Rochalle sat on one side, and though she was close to them she heard not a word of what they were saying. She heard something else—sweet sounds totally unlike the words that were being exchanged between Freidel and Dvossa-Malka. She was listening to the glorious outpourings of Stempenyu's heart as they were expressed in the fiddle. They penetrated to the depths of her soul at once. She felt like rooted to the spot so long as the music continued. She only stirred when it ceased, and when Stempenyu was standing in the door of his room. Their eyes met, and they both grew red as fire. Stempenyu remained where he was. He did not move an inch one way or the other. He was like a statue. And, Rochalle looked at him in silence. She said to her mother-in-law that it was time to go home. Dvossa-Malka caught on at once. She wrung her hands and exclaimed:

"May a thunder strike me! See how we have been carried away with our talk. Well, what will you take from me for the corals, Freidel? You must not charge me dear, Freidel. With me you ought to deal as with a business woman."

"On my word of honor, Dvossa-Malka—may I be choked as with the first bite I eat if I am telling you a lie—I had to pay eighteen *roubles* myself for that row of corals; but, Dvossa-Malka, I will let you have them for fifteen *roubles*.

"Fifteen! Rubbish! Fifteen! I will give you twelve *roubles*, cash down."

"Oh, may you be strong and healthy, Dvossa-Malka," was Freidel's answer, speaking with much warmth, and taking Dvossa-Malka by both hands, as women take hold of one another when they are going to dance.

Meanwhile, Rochalle and Stempenyu took advantage of the opportunity they now had to exchange a few words.

"I wish to say something to you, Stempenyu."

"And I wish to say something to you, Rochalle."

"You have said it already."

"When?"

"In your letter."

"It was too little."

"It was too much."

"No, not by a hundredth part too much."

"You are mistaken."

"I swear to you by my life. Where can I see you?"

"I do not know where we can meet."

"Perhaps one evening."

"Where?"

"On the Monastery Road."

"What time?"

"On Saturday evening. You will come from the other side of the monastery garden."

"I cannot, I will not."

"You must, Rochalle. I beg of you to come and meet me for a minute. Be thou there. I will be there surely. Saturday evening without fail, Rochalle."

"I will not be there."

"You *will* be there, Rochalle—you will."

"Well daughter," put in Dvossa-Malka at this juncture, "let us go home. Come! I have just managed to get the corals for fourteen *roubles*. Oh, I never thought that Freidel was such a keen business woman."

"Oh, Dvossa-Malka, God preserve you! You know how to secure a bargain. I wish you a good day. Go in peace! Wear it in peace! Use it in peace, and break it in peace!"

* * *

"To the devil with her! How she excited me!" said Freidel to Stempenyu, as she stood near him after having closed the door behind Rochalle and Dvossa-Malka. "And, she, the daughter-in-law—the white devil—sat quite still and silent. And, the corals suited her as a nose ring suits a swine!"

When Rochalle arrived home with the string of corals still hanging about her neck, where Freidel had put them, her mother-in-law, Dvossa-Malka, brought her over to Isaac-Naphtali, with a smile of satisfaction, as if she had just achieved goodness only knew what victory.

"What do you say to these corals, Isaac-Naphtali?" she asked. "They are a bargain—a real bargain!"

Isaac-Naphtali poked his head forward so that he might scrutinize the corals with greater care—with the alert eyes of a connoisseur. He sniffed with an air of mild caution and asked:

"What did you pay for them? How much?"

"Guess. Give a guess. You consider yourself a judge—then guess," said Dvossa-Malka, smiling at him significantly.

"I don't know whether you mean me to say how

cheap or how dear they were."

"Didn't I tell you I bought them at a bargain, fool? A desperate bargain. You can just imagine that they were a bargain when I tell you that I had to sweat and toil before I got them out of that terrible Freidel, the wife of the musician. She knows how to fight for a *kopek*. The devil only knows where she learned how to do it. And, she has a tongue that is like sulfur and brimstone. And, when she is talking to a customer she wails and weeps—the devil take her—the Stempenyu woman! Nu! Speak, Isaac Naphtali. Let me hear your verdict! Well, why are you silent? Tell me what you think these corals ought to cost."

"What these corals ought to have cost you, you want to know," was Isaac-Naphtali's reply, as he took the ends of his beard and bit them between his teeth. They ought to have cost you—wait, let me try to guess accurately. I do not want to make a fool of myself. You said a bargain—didn't you? If you got them a bargain you ought to have paid for them no less than six and a half *roubles*. But, they are worth the whole seven.

"Idiot!" shrieked Dvossa-Malka in a voice that was loud as cannon-shot. At this Isaac-Naphtali took fright and shrunk away to one side. "You idiot! You beast with a horse's face! A row of corals like this for six and a half *roubles*. Mad fool! A dumb creature would not have uttered such stupid words in a year as you who can speak have uttered just now. Have you got eyes or have you not? Here! Look at them again, you fool! You plucked idiot you!"

And, Dvossa-Malka took Rochalle by the hand and led her over to Isaac-Naphtali. She lifted Rochalle's head so that the corals might be seen all the plainer. And, while Isaac-Naphtali was examining them for the second time, she thrust at him again and again with her biting sarcasm. Isaac-Naphtali, poor man! only sniffed hard and blinked his eyes. He was afraid to say a word. But, Heaven had pity on him, and at that moment sent in Moshe-Mendel, stick in hand. He had just come from the market, and was still full of bargains and bargaining. Without a moment's hesitation, he took to valuing the corals which were hanging around Rochalle's beautiful white throat. He said that they must have cost, at the very least, three *roubles*, at which Dvossa-Malka was so enraged that she burst out crying like a little child. No one had appreciated the wonderful bargain she had secured at such great pains. And, it may be that she cried also because of the heartache which had smitten her at the thought she had been fooled by Freidel.

"You are indeed a clever merchant," she said at last to Moshe-Mendel. "You are quite as clever as that father of yours. Why three *roubles*? Why not less?"

"Because they are worth no more. Because the corals are poor in quality. I have seen corals, mother—I've seen a fine lot of strings of corals, I can tell you. And I know."

And, throughout the whole of that day the three of them fought and argued and disputed about the value of the corals.

"If he had short me in the heart with a pistol," wailed Dvossa-Malka, "I should not have been so hurt as I was when I heard the words, 'six and a half'! Let it be that the woman did fool me. (And nobody has ever fooled me yet.) Let it be that she did fool me! May she and Stempenyu together have a black year! But, what good is it to throw salt on another's wounds? What good has it done him that he came out with 'six and a half'? May she have six and a half dozen wounds on her body! I will get back from her my money, if I have to drag it out of her as one drags a bone from the mouth of a dog! But, just picture to yourself how he had the heart—the check to bring himself to say, 'six and a half'!"

* * *

The whole scene was so despicable to Rochalle that she snatched off the corals the very instant she found herself alone in her own room. And, she made up her mind that she would never wear them again as long as she lived. More than all, she was annoyed with Moshe-Mendel because he had been so much taken up with the value of the corals that he had never even looked at her or taken notice of her, thought he looked at the corals that were around her neck with great care. He never even said to her, after the usual custom, "Rochalle, I wish you well to wear them!" The three of them had dragged her backwards and forwards all day long, looking at the corals, just as if they could not have examined them if she had taken them off. They seemed to regard her as of no more value than a cow that one takes to the market. Each of them in turn went over to her and raised her head, and felt the corals, and scrutinized them with narrow eyes. But, they all forgot about Rochalle herself. Though she was not by nature either hot tempered or ill-natured, she stormed inwardly at everybody, especially at Moshe-Mendel who afterwards took his supper with the utmost unconcern. Then he went off to the House of Learning, where there was a meeting, from which he did not return till the small hours of the morning, as had happened with him many times before.

Rochalle was very excited. Her face was aflame, her head was dizzy, and in her ears was a hissing and a singing. She did not know what had come over her. And, to crown her suffering, Dvossa-Malka was standing over her, and driving her mad with questions. She was pressing her to eat and drink, and was not satisfied with Rochalle's refusals, but demanded to know the why and the wherefore. But, Rochalle refused to eat or drink, and also refused to open her lips. When she found herself alone, at last, she had a good cry. Later on, when she got into bed, it was only to weep afresh. The tears gushed from her eyes in a torrent—warm, hot tears that seemed as if they would never cease to fall.

XXI   A HEAVY NIGHT

What was Rochalle weeping for? She did not know why she was weeping. She hardly knew that she wept. Her heart had been heavy for some time past—very heavy; and now, at the first opportunity, it seemed to overflow, and to send forth a stream of tears. She felt so lonely, and sad, and forsaken. She wanted something, but she did not know what, nor could she know. In reflecting on everything connecting with her past life, she had to admit that her parents had married her off in order to get rid of her. And, the word "rid" was in itself sufficient to bring the tears to her eyes all over again.

It is a word which is used very often amongst us Jews, and in nearly every family. It is a shameful word, and carries in itself the essence of all that is most strongly opposed to the spirit of our glorious faith which is founded on compassion and kindness.

But, more than all, Rochalle was heartily sick of Moshe-Mendel, and his ways, and his attitude towards her. She realized to the full what part she was playing in his life, despite of her beauty and her goodness, and her honesty. She saw now clearly, and for the first time, what she was to him.

Then, too, she herself had been confused and harassed and excited of late. It was of no trifling matter what she had had to endure through the importunities of Stempenyu. The pious, God-fearing Rochalle, who had never wished and never dared to ignore the most insignificant Jewish law or custom relating to the conduct of women—the same Rochalle who had most positively based her life on the books of Faith which were especially written for Jewish women—she now carried about in her heart the image of a strange man, received letters and met with him, without a single pang of conscience. On the contrary she felt herself being drawn towards Stempenyu, more and more. She wished to see him, to talk with him, and to listen to him as he played his fiddle. Oh, how he played! She felt that she would be quite satisfied not to eat and not to sleep anymore, if she could only go on listening to him, and if she were sure of seeing him always. His eyes, when they fell on her, seemed to warm her, and at the same time to soothe and to fascinate her! Ah, those burning eyes of his!

Rochalle caught hold of her head in both hands, and gave herself up to listening to the throbbing of her temples and to the beating of her heart.

And, her soul was being drawn from her—and drawn. She did not know what had come over her. She covered her head with the bedclothes, and the next instant she was filled with a strange feeling that her old friend of long ago was standing over her—her old companion, Chaya-Ettel—peace be unto her!

And, as she ran mentally over the whole sad story of Chaya-Ettel's brief life-her bitter disappointments, and the treachery of Benjamin—a cold shudder past over Rochalle's frame.

When she lifted the covers off her head, at last, her ears were assailed by a familiar melody, played in a similar fashion on a well-known fiddle. She thought at first that she only imagined she heard the sounds, as she had imagined she saw Chaya-Ettel; but, the longer she listened, the more she became convinced that the sounds were real. And, what was more, they were closer to her each moment. A popular air was being played, such as the musicians were in the habit of playing to accompany to their homes the wedding guests after the supper— those who were so closely related to the bridegroom that they were privileged to remain behind after the other guests, in the house of the bride, carrying on the rejoicings for some time afterwards, perhaps for two or three days on end.

Rochalle, on recognizing the melody, had no difficulty ion deciding why it was being played, and by whom. She knew that it was Stempenyu and his orchestra escorting the bridegroom's relatives back to their homes, at the other end of the village, and playing for them as they marched along.

But, she could not think for whom they were playing. The wedding of Chayam-Benzion's daughter was almost forgotten. Whom, then, were the musicians leading back to their homes? There was no one else getting married.

Rochalle was sure of that. But, what did it mean that Stempenyu was out with his orchestra at such an hour of the night? There was no doubt that he had his full orchestra with him; for, she heard distinct sounds of the drum and the cymbals. And, they were drawing nearer and nearer to her. They were playing very nicely. But, out above all the other instruments, she could hear the sounds of Stempenyu's fiddle. Though its tones were sweet and soft and sentimental, Rochalle could hear it as clearly as if all the other instruments were hushed and muffled. She could not lie still. She jumped up and rushed over to the window, and leant out, nearly halfway through.

It was a long time since Rochalle had seen such a beautiful night. The moon was riding high in the heavens, and around her were scattered a myriad of stars in clusters—diamonds which sparkled and shimmered before her eyes in ten thousand colours. The air was fresh and balmy. Not a breeze stirred, so that the huge beech trees of the monastery garden were like so many sentinels keeping guard. Not a leaf nor a twig moved. Only at odd intervals the pungent odour of the beeches were wafted from the garden to Rochalle's nostrils as she stood at the lattice. It was as if a great bunch of sweet-smelling herbs had been placed beside her.

And, the sweet odour was all the more welcome to her because, in the daytime, quite a different odour filled the atmosphere.

Rochalle was almost equal in beauty with the wondrous beauty of the night—the snow-white, pure-hearted Rochalle, with her blue eyes like stars, and her long golden hair falling about her shoulders like a mantle.

(Did Rochalle remember, or did it strike her at all, that the author of this book, as well as the moon and the stars, was looking at the beautiful locks of golden hair, which to all the world were kept hidden completely out of sight under a silk cap?)

Her eyes were no less blue than the morning sky at its clearest. And, her shining face was not less radiant than the star-lit night. But, Rochalle hardly thought of anything like that—anything like the comparison of her own beauty of what lay around her. Her thoughts were not with herself at al. They were far off, following the direction whence came the sweet sounds. And, her heart went out to Stempenyu, and his fiddle.

The orchestra was playing a very sad air. It was as if someone had just been laid to rest under the sod, in a lonely grave.

It has been so with us always. Our feastings, our rejoicings, have always found their most adequate expression in tears and weeping. Through an excess of joy, our hearts are melted, as with sorrow.

But, the melody sounded lonelier and more melancholy now as it came out over the still night air, when the whole village was sunken in sleep. Only a small number of persons heard the weeping music—the persons who were returning from the wedding with drooping heads. Why were they so silent? You see, they had got rid of a child—that is, provided for its future. Thanks be to the Holy Name! And, in the stillness of the summer night Stempenyu's fiddle was heard far better than at any other time. One's heart sank within one, and the soul was drawn out of one's body. The very roots of one's life seemed as if they were about to be torn out by the sweetness of the melody.

And, Rochalle stood in the window, half naked, listening and listening. She thought that she ought to run away, and close the window tight so that she should not hear any more; but, she could not move from the spot. She was like one petrified—like a steel that cannot withstand the power of the magnet. She continued to look about her, and to bend her ear to listen. She felt that she was not listening to his fiddle, but to himself. And, he was begging her, pleading with her, weeping before her.

Rochalle was not the only being who was listening to Stempenyu in surprise, on this warm, soft night. The moon and the stars and the air itself—all nature seemed to have relapsed into a dead silence in order to listen the more attentively to Stempenyu. And, there were others who, on the contrary, woke up to listen to him, who stood up to hear what sort of peculiar unknown sounds were disturbing the night. What did it mean that the quiet night was interrupted in this fashion? The cock that woke the whole village with his crowing at the dawn of day was led into imagining that he had overslept himself, and that the night had passed already. He got down from his perch, flapped his wings, crowed aloud and went back to his nest again. Seeing that it was not daylight at all yet, he felt aggrieved that he had been disturbed for nothing.

Even the dogs—the watch-dogs of the monastery—on hearing the Jewish orchestra in the middle of the night, began to bark, as they were in the habit of doing. But they, too, grew silent when they found that nothing further happened. They sought out their kennels, and fell asleep. And, the cow—Dvossa-Malka's treasure—set its ears and listened to the unwonted sounds. It let out a deep bellow that was like a groan. And, its neighbors, two goats, jumped up from the straw they were lying on, and ran into one another to show off their horns.

In short, everything grew lively at the sound of the fiddle on this calm and beautiful night—on this warm summer's night that was full of charm and mystery.

Rochalle did not move all the time that the fiddle was still to be heard. She felt that she was bound to the spot with iron clamps. And she was lost in wonder and amazement. She forgot completely where she was. She only felt that she was surrounded by the beauties of the night. And, what a night it was, heavenly Father! As she stood there all her senses were on the alert to drink in every note and every breeze of the mild air hat was wafted to her. She was like one in a dream, enchanted. She looked up at the blue of the sky, and she was reminded of the summer nights of long ago when she was a little child and sat on the door-step, and counted the stars, and followed the moonbeams as they spread here and there. And, she used to sing to herself the little song which was so popular at that time:

"The moon is shining on the night,
And Perralle sits at her door.
She sighs, and moans, and pines away,
Her heart is filled with grief.
She sighs, and moans, and pines away,
Her heart is filled with grief!"

At that time Rochalle did not understand the real meaning of the song, though she sand it over and over again, times without number. But, she understood it now. She felt the full force of its message and its pathos. And she felt also, now that her emotions were stirred out of their slumber, that there was something which was drawing her hence—out into the night, into the free air and under the vast blue sky over her head. She felt that it was too hot for her in the house, and too narrow and too uncomfortable. And, then there came into her mind another song from her old repertory, which she thought she had long forgotten—another of those that she used to connect with the silver moonlight, and which she always sang at night on the door-step, when she was a little child:

"I stand on the brink of the river;
But cannot get over to thee.
Oh, I long to go, but I cannot—
I cannot get over to thee.
Oh, I long to go, but I cannot—
I cannot get over to thee!"

Stempenyu had now come quite close to her. There he was with his fiddle and his long hair and his blazing, burning eyes that seemed to be looking at her always—warming her with their piercing glances and with the fire that was always burning in them. She felt that it would have been the greatest satisfaction of her life to be near him always, and to listen to him for ever and ever, as she was listening now. Then, too, she would have liked to keep looking back into his burning black eyes, into them always and for ever. . . .

But there was one thing which Rochalle could not

understand. How did Stempenyu come here? What did he want here, at dead of night, with his fiddle? Was he not taking the wedding guests a long way around? That was what she could not make out, no matter how much she puzzled her brain with the problem. It occurred to her at last that a wedding had taken place at a synagogue that day. But, how came the guests to be in the far-off corner of the village in which she lived?

It was only at that instant that she began to see the light—to understand the secret—on the moment when Stempenyu and his orchestra were close beside her window, almost at the door of her house. Stempenyu came forward, and began to play a solo with much vivacity and spirit. Then it was that Rochalle understood everything—why he had dragged all the wedding guests, as well as the orchestra around the village, a dozen streets away from their destination. And, for whom had he done this bold thing? She felt that he was paying her a high compliment, and her heart was filled with pleasurable sensations. It leaped up within her so that she thought it would fly out of her bosom altogether. She never thought for a moment that he was compromising her. She was only glad of that compliment that he was paying her. Unconsciously, unwittingly, she began to laugh softly within herself—a joyous, mirthful laugh that betokened her deep sense of pleasure and satisfaction. But, she was startled at the sound of her own voice. She was wide awake now, and saw herself as she was, standing in the window, in the scantest attire, her head thrust forward and her hair flying loose about her shoulders. She darted from the window, and jumped back into bed. "Ah, woe is me! Ah, woe is me!" she murmured. "See to what a pass one can come if one does not consider beforehand what one is about, and where one is in the world. There was I, in the window, at dead of night, only half-dressed, a crowd of men around me, and my mind completely filled with foolish, empty nonsense. More than that! I carry about in my heart the most sinful thoughts, and am filled with pictures, not of my husband, but of Stempenyu. And Stempenyu? He has a cheek to drag a crowd of Jews over the half the village for nothing. One must have a fine set of nerves that permit one to do such a thing. Where did he get the idea? I must ask him. And, I must make an end to this sort of thing, once and for always. He wants to bring about my ruin. I will talk the whole business over with him, and tell him exactly what I think of him. What is it that they say about the first quarrel being better than—something or another—I forget what. He tells me a whole yarn about love. Rubbish! It's a good joke, as I live! 'Next Saturday evening,' he says, 'on the Monastery Road, there he will explain everything to me.' I wish the Sabbath would come quicker, so that I might not be kept long waiting to tell him what I think of him. And, at the same time, to hear what he has to say. I will surely go. What have I to be afraid of? Whom do I care about? One has no right to be afraid of any person—of anyone but the Lord himself.

"Stempenyu is a nuisance; but, I will make an end of everything. It's not for nothing that there are so many stories told about him. But, what has it to do with me? Why should I waste my young years bothering about him? And, who is to blame for everything if not I myself? One must never permit the least liberty. If Moshe-Mendel were here, he would have told Stempenyu a thing or two. But, where is he? A lot he cares what happens to me! What is it to him that I am annoyed, in pain almost? Ah, but what good is all this? I had better say my night's prayer. It is wrong to fall asleep without saying it:

" 'For Thy Salvation have I hoped, O Lord! I have hoped, O Lord, for Thy Salvation! O Lord, for Thy Salvation have I hoped!' "

Rochalle buried her head in the pillows, and drew up the cover as high as possible, so that she might not hear the playing of the orchestra. And, she repeated aloud: "For Thy Salvation have I hoped, O Lord!"

But, through the open window stole the sweet strains of Stempeyu's fiddle—the strains that were growing softer and fainter and more remote. And, again Rochalle repeated the lines from the night prayer:

"For Thy Salvation have I hoped, O Lord! I have hoped, O Lord, for Thy Salvation! O Lord, for Thy Salvation have I hoped!"

And, Stempenyu's fiddle sounded still further off, until its tones were barely audible. At last they died away altogether.... Gradually Rochalle's eyes were closing in sleep. Her lips hardly moved. The whispered lines were dying into a faint blue murmur: "For Thy Salvation.... For Thy Salvation...."

And, Rochalle was fast asleep.

Rochalle fell asleep, and dreamt that Stempenyu was fastening a row of corals around her neck. On one side of her stood her father-in-law, wearing his phylacteries and praying shawl; and, Freidel was beating him, was smacking his face for him, as furiously as she could. Moshe-Mendel was dead drunk, and was riding on a pony, and making it perform all sorts of tricks, while Stempenyu was still hanging the corals around her neck. On the other side of her stood Chaya-Ettel, dressed in her Sabbath clothes. She was covered with the most beautiful jewels, like a "Queen's Daughter," and she was smiling pleasantly and kindly, as she went on lighting a number of candles one after the other.

"What are you doing, Chaya-Ettel?" asked Rochalle. 'Why are you lighting so many candles?"

"What a question!" answered Chaya-Ettel, with a little laugh. "Isn't it the Sabbath eve, and quite time to light the Sabbath candles?"

Rochalle looked at the candles. How brightly and clearly they were burning. And all the time Stempenyu was still hanging the corals around her neck. He was standing so close to her that she could hear his breath coming and going. He was staring straight into her eyes. And, again his glances seemed to warm her through and through. She was delighted with herself. She laughed joyously and sang. And Stempenyu was still hanging the corals about her neck.

Suddenly the lights were extinguished, and all those who had stood around her had disappeared. It grew pitch dark and very cold, as in a cellar or in a grave. The wind blew and whistled, and there arose a sad and mournful sound—a wailing chant. The sound of a fiddle was also to be heard—the familiar sounds played on Stempenyu's fiddle. Stempenyu himself was gone, but his fiddle was still to be heard. And, it was terribly sad and lonely. It was like the sound of someone weeping.... It was Chaya Ettel weeping for her lost youth, for the days which had fled from her as if they were no more than a dream. She was weeping, too, after her lover, Benjamin, who had given her up for another woman—who had forgotten all the vows he had made to love her forever. He had forgotten her completely.

"Oh, mother!" cried Rochalle, wakening up with a start. But, in the next moment she had turned over on her side and was fast asleep again, only to continue the dream which had visited her before. The whole night she was completely entangled in her dreams, in which Stempenyu was always standing near her and trying to hang around her neck the inevitable row of corals. And, yet again Chaya-Ettel came forward, carrying the black candles and weeping and moaning, and sobbing and repeating from the prayer-book the words: "Almighty Father in Heaven! All-Powerful Creator! Lord of all Flesh! King of all kings, who from everlasting until everlasting art the One God! Let my prayers be acceptable unto Thee! Let the petition of my heart find favour in Thy eyes. Let the prayers of the upright be heard, and their petitions fulfilled! Behold! They prostrate themselves before Thy footstool! They beseech of Thee Thy mercy for all created beings as well as for themselves. They seek of Thee forgiveness; for, everything that is upon the earth is full of sin!"

Chaya-Ettel was repeating the words aloud, and weeping and moaning in the most pitiful accents, between each word....

A little later, and she was gone.

In the village of Tasapevka there was a monastery. It had been built, according to legend, by the national here, Mazeppa. A high, white stone wall encircled the monastery on all sides. And, the ground that the monastery and its garden covered was equal in size to about three-fourths of the area of the village itself. Facing one wall were the shops and the warehouses of the village. At another wall were built a number of underground passages and cellars in which had hidden long ago a whole army of Haidemaks; but, now they were used for storing away apples and other thing which need to be kept in a cold place. The third wall was covered with thorns and briars, and was overhung with poplars and other trees which grew in the monastery garden, on the other side of the wall. The fourth wall was bare and smooth. In several places there were holes, where the mortar had fallen out from between the bricks, loosening them. The wall had cried out for repairs years ago, but had been neglected. And, opposite this wall, with only the roadway intervening, there stood a group of houses and wooden *isbas*, farmsteads and villas, occupied by Jews as well as Christians, in about equal proportions. The little road upon which the houses stood, and which was bounded by the dead wall of the monastery, was called the Monastery Road. And, there at the corner of the road, where the first clump of trees overhung the wall, there took place the first meeting between Rochalle and Stempenyu.

The reader, who has probably been accustomed to highly interesting romances, has surely been tortured enough in reading this romance down to this particular point in the narrative, for it contains neither stirring scenes nor extraordinary happenings. No one was shot, and no one was poisoned. And neither dukes nor earls have come upon the stage, so to speak. All the characters are the most ordinary, commonplace folks of everyday life—commonplace men, ordinary musicians, and plain women of rather course grain. And, the reader is probably waiting for the Sabbath evening to come round, when will be enacted the great melodramatic scene—the romantic meeting between the hero and the heroine on the Monastery Road. But, I must say in advance that the expectation is in vain. There took place no melodramatic scene; because Rochalle did not come here after the fashion of an abandoned woman—not at all like one of those wicked women of highly spiced romances who runs to kiss her lover in secret in every dark corner. No such thing! Rochalle only wanted to see Stempenyu in order to ask him how he—a mere musician—had the audacity to write her such a letter? How he dared to forget for a moment that she was the daughter-in-law of Isaac-Naphtali, and the wife of Moshe-Mendel?

"I must prevent the like from ever happening again," she said to herself. "I will tell him what I think of him once and for all. How does the saying go, 'Better the first tiff than the last quarrel!'"

That thought did not come to her suddenly. Rochalle had time all the week, and especially on the Sabbath day, to think of everything. And oh, what she had suffered on that last day! What a terrible struggle she had had with the Spirit of Evil—with temptation. No, the name of the Spirit of Evil hardly fits in here. How could it come near her—near such a good woman, a pure and virtuous woman? How could she be connected with such a fearful person as the Spirit of Evil? How could he come near to a woman like Rochalle who had never read a romance in her life, and who knew nothing at all about love affairs, excepting the one story of Chaya-Ettel—peace be unto her! How could she come to be struggling with the Evil One? Love? Nonsense! If she were not married it might have been different. She would then have been, as they say, a free bird, her head unadorned with the matron's cap—an individual for herself. But, a married woman—and a pious woman into the bargain, of good family, full of pride—she herself stood in the way of doing what was wrong. Her own conscience was aflame with righteous indignation. She thought that she had already committed a great wrong, and felt that she could never again lift her head for shame. She wandered about the house, finding no place for herself. Now she lay down on her bed, and again she rushed out in the open air; for it seemed to her as if she were choking—as if she could not draw her breath. And, then she was overcome with a curious feeling, as if her soul could not hold itself within her, but was trying to make its escape out into the broad world. In distraction, she betook herself to the Bible. She opened the book at random, and her eyes fell upon the following passage:

"And Dinah the daughter of Leah,... went out to see the daughters of the land.

"And when Shechem the son of Hamor saw her... he took her." And, the commentary added, "Shechem persuaded her."

Rochalle went on reading from the Bible which Dvossa-Malka had given her for a present before she was married. She forgot, by degrees, that she was reading. Her imagination took hold of the story, and her thoughts wandered off, carrying her away towards Stempenyu, to the Monastery Road, under the beech trees, where he promised to wait for her.... He was surely waiting there.

No sooner did Stempenyu come into her mind than she felt drawn towards him, as if he were a magnet and influenced her movements. She did not understand her own heart, and her own weakness.

"I should like to ask him only this," she repeated a dozen times, for her own personal satisfaction. "I should like to know what I am to him that he should bother me in this way. What does he want of me?"

And, again Rochalle remembered her comrade, Chaya-Ettel—peace be unto her! And all that she had suffered through the falseness of Benjamin....

But, Benjamin had been Chaya-Ettel's own cousin

and foster-brother; and, at the time when she fell in love with Benjamin, she was not married, neither was he. Whilst she, Rochalle, was another man's wife when Stempenyu came into the road; and, he too was married. Oh, how terrible it was to knock up against such hard facts as these! She shuddered at the thought of them.

And he, Stempenyu? He was no more than a wandering musician. Why did he get in her way? What was he to her that he should write her letters? Surely, he had no right whatever to do any such thing. The cheek of him— the cheek of that good-for-nothing!

"If the world were to turn upside down," she said to herself repeatedly, "if the world were to turn itself upside down, I must see him, and must tell him what I think of him. Why should I be afraid of him? I will see him—I will see him without fail. No one will see me. I will steal out for a minute. It is not far. It is only over the road. I shall be home again before they miss me."

And, Rochalle looked through the open window, on the Monastery Road, and saw the trees—the tall beeches and poplars as they stood erect in all their pride and glory. And, she heard the songs of the birds that had their nests in the branches. How beautifully they sang from out the garden! Rochalle's fanciful thoughts, her fantasies, went out yonder, where, in an hour, or perhaps less she would talk to Stempenyu and see him, eye to eye. And, she felt her heart beating wildly within her. She was breathing heavily, as if a great struggle were going on within her. And, the truth—the truth must be told—was that the minutes were terribly long to her. She could hardly contain herself. She wished that it were evening already. She counted the minutes until her father-in-law and her husband came back from the evening prayer at the synagogue, and when her mother-in-law would change her Sabbath dress for her everyday one, and begin to fuss around the *somovar*, and heat the oven, to make the great Saturday night supper, at which there were always a houseful of visitors. Then would come the moment when she, Rochalle, would throw a shawl about her shoulders and steal out, quietly, through the door, and into the street, as if she were going for a walk. Who would notice that she was going to—? Where? Her limbs trembled and her cheeks were aflame. And her heart? Oh, her heart was almost throbbing out of her body. As the minutes went by, she felt herself being drawn more and more to the spot where Stempenyu was waiting for her, until she could think of no one and nothing else.

She did not see what lay about her. She saw only the trees of the monastery garden—only Stempenyu with his great blazing eyes like two living coals. She heard nothing. The murmur of voices about her did not reach her. She was listening to an imaginary sound—to the sweet melodies that came forth from the little fiddle, at the touch of Stempenyu's hand.

Rochalle was entirely filled with one desire—to see Stempenyu and to be near him. She thought only of him.

And, she felt that there was nothing in the whole world which could hinder her, or prevent her from carrying out what she wished to do from the very bottom of her heart—from going to meet Stempenyu.

XXIII THE FIRE BURNS BUT IS SOON EXTINGUISHED

No sooner had the dusk fallen, than Stempenyu hurried off with his orchestra to play for a special dance which a number of the girls of the village were getting up in honour of one of their comrades who was about to get married in a few days. He took his fiddle under his arm so that Freidel might be led to think that he, too, was going to play at the dance. The moment he was out of sight of the house he gave his fiddle to Michsa Drummer, and betook himself in all haste to the Monastery Road, where he walked up and down under the shadow of trees. He looked about him carefully every few minutes, in the direction in which the beautiful Rochalle lived. That she would come he never doubted in the least. Every nerve in his body thrilled at the prospect of her coming; and, he had seen it plainly in her eyes at the time when he had met her in his own house, whither she had come to buy corals of Freidel.

Stempenyu was not mistaken. No more than a quarter of an hour after he had arrived on the scene, his eyes fell on the figure of a woman on the other side of the street, gliding along rapidly, and turning around now and again to see if there was no one in sight. She wore a white shawl over her head and shoulders, and drawn down so tightly until it almost covered her eyes as well. Her hands were trembling and her teeth were chattering, and her heart within her bosom was palpitating wildly. Her whole body was as in a fever. When she came near to Stempenyu she looked hard at him before she stopped. The next moment she was beside him, crying out: "Where did you get the impudence? How dare you?"

"Don't say 'you,' Rochalle; say 'thou,'" answered Stempenyu, as he took hold of her two hands, and fixed his black eyes on her blue ones. Rochalle noticed that his eyes had in them exactly the same sort of glitter as the stars that were looking down at them from the blue vault of the heavens, through the balmy evening air.

All the Jews of the village were now singing the Saturday evening's "Elijah," and sighing after the usual fashion. The were thoughtful and abstracted, worrying their heads, once again, after the day's respite, over the problems of their livelihood, and wishing they had the good luck which had once attended a Jew who had come face to face with the dispenser of all good—Elijah the prophet, who had wished the Jew peace himself, in answer to the Jew's greeting of "Peace be unto you!"

The women had already taken off their Sabbath caps and gowns and ornaments, and had betaken themselves to their ordinary tasks. In a word, the whole village of

Tasapevka was speeding the parting guest—the Holy Sabbath. And, no one dreamt that that in the same hour, Rochalle, Dvossa-Malka's daughter-in-law, was keeping a clandestine appointment with the musician Stempenyu on the Monastery Road, and that they were holding a conversation which was miles removed from Jewishness and Judaism. But, the bright stars that were looking down, and the tall trees that grew in the garden, and the night birds that had their nests in the trees and were calling to each other in a language of their own—these knew, and heard, and saw everything. They alone knew that on this enchanting night, under the monastery trees, on the street of the Gentiles and by the side of Stempenyu, Rochalle found herself in an entirely new situation—so much so that she had forgotten everything about herself, who and what she was. Here in the delicious fragrance of the night, and surrounded by the stillness of Mother Nature herself, Rochalle felt as she had never felt before in all her life. The terror which had fallen upon her in the first moments had now left her completely, and in its place she experienced the curious feeling that she had somehow developed wings, and that she was free, and might lift up her wings and fly if she wished it.

Stempenyu drew closer to her, and put his two arms around her waste. Rochalle trembled at his touch. She wished to walk away from him, but she did not stir. She looked hard at Stempenyu, and the tears began to gather in her beautiful eyes.

"What are you crying for?" asked Stempenyu, wiping the tears from her cheeks.

"Oh, Stempenyu, I feel so happy being near you— here beside you. Stempenyu, why am I...? Why am I not...?"

"Why are you not mine, you would ask? You are mine, Rochalle. You are mine."

"Stempenyu, how can that be? What do you mean by saying I am yours?"

"You are mine, don't you see, heart of me! You are mine because I am yours always and for ever. To the dark tomb, to the grave itself, I am yours, life of my life."

"Benjamin said the same and also took an oath. Yet what was the result?"

"What Benjamin?" asked Stempenyu, wondering at her meaning, and hazing in her eyes, as one gazes into the eyes of a little child after it has said something very foolish. "What Benjamin are you talking about?"

"Benjamin—Chaya-Ettel's cousin. My friend Chaya-Ettel—peace be unto her!—had a cousin whose name was Benjamin. He swore that he was hers for ever and ever. He swore by all that is pure and holy, by his very soul. And in the end? Ah, she had a sad end, poor Chaya-Ettel. She died a good while ago—peace be unto her! I ask her pardon for speaking so lightly of her. But, Benjamin was the very life of her. She would have been satisfied to die at his feet. She told me so herself. I can see her standing as clearly before my eyes as if she were still alive. I imagined often that she and I are sitting in the open window, and I am singing my little songs for her, and she is weeping. She lifts up her head every now and again, and says to me: "Oh, Rochalle, do not believe any of them. Men are all false, every one of them."

Rochalle went on talking of her dead friend, Chaya-Ettel, the orphan girl, while Stempenyu was kissing her hands, embracing her, and gazing in fond raptures at her beautiful face. Rochalle told him everything about Chaya-Ettel, even to the manner of her death—how she had faded away like a candle, in silence, for love of her darling Benjamin. Though she was dead now some time, Rochalle remembered her quite distinctly. She had thought of her frequently, and dreamt of her often. And, as she was speaking, it seemed to her that Chaya-Ettel was standing on the top of the high monastery wall, dressed in her white grave-clothes. She seemed to Rochalle to be looking directly at her, and winking in the direction of Stempenyu significantly. She also shook her head sadly and doubtfully, as one would say, had see had the power:

"What are you doing here, Rochalle?"

"What good is it, Rochalle, my life—what good is it to you to talk, and think of such things, especially at night? Rather than look at me with your luminous eyes that shine and sparkle like two beautiful diam—"

Stempenyu had no time to finish the word. Rochalle tore herself from his embrace with such force that he was afraid of her.

"God be with you, Rochalle! What is the matter?" He tried to put his arms around her again, but she would not let him. She trembled and sighed.

"Can't you see? She is—look! She is standing there! She is looking this way—this way!"

"Who is standing? Where? What are you saying, Rochalle? My soul, come to me. Take my hand...."

"Let me be, Stempenyu, let me be. Don't you see her? There is something white on the wall. Oh, it is she—it is she. It is Chaya-Ettel! Oh, leave me alone—leave me alone! What do you mean by your impudence?

What do you mean? I should like to know that! I wish you a good-night—a good-night!"

Hardly were the words out of her mouth, than she rushed away and disappeared in the dark shadows cast by the trees. Stempenyu could only see the two ends of her white shawl as they fluttered behind her like two wings.

So vanishes one's better angel—so disappears the last trace of a pleasant dream when the morning has come with one's awakening!

Oh, daughter of Israel, now you have shown your virtues, your purity of heart, your strength in the time of temptation—the whole innocence of your Jewish soul! Here, when the hour of your trial was at hand, you showed your faithfulness and your sincerity!

* * *

When she found herself at home, Rochalle was strongly tempted to shout aloud at the top of her voice, so that everybody might hear, of all that she had done and said and where she had been and with whom. But, she found that the family was not alone. A large number of guests were seated around the hissing *samovar*. They were deeply absorbed in a discussion about the principles of the business they occupied themselves with, severally. This was what people usually argued about on Saturday nights in Jewish houses, in Russian villages. They generally came together in groups after the day's rest, and talked and argued about the state of trade—about the fairs of the next day, and about ordinary, everyday matters which they had expelled from their thoughts during the Sabbath, as being unsuited for the holy day of rest.

"I will not take my goods to the fair!" cried a stout Jew, a linen draper. "Let the fair go to the devil. I know quite enough about fairs. They only annoy and aggravate one. They eat the heart out of one's body. That's all the good they ever bring to anyone."

"Why so?" asked Dvossa-Malka, folding her hands across her ample bosom. "I don't know who you can say that? I wonder, Reb Youdel, why you are angry with fairs? Last week your stall was crowded with customers. I wish that all good men did as much business as you have done. I am sure you got in a lot of money."

"To you everything is getting in money!" interposed Isaac-Naphtali, without even looking in the direction in which his wife was standing.

"And, I hope that we may never have a worse day than we had last Sunday," said Moshe-Mendel, lifting his head from his account-book. "Why one should set out to belittle the fair, and to deny that it was a good fair, is more than I can make out."

"Ah, that is the reason," replied Youdel. "You never believe anyone else. When you see ten peasants coming into one's booth together you at once imagine that there is a great deal of business going on. You will not believe that it is no such thing, and that the peasants only rob one right and left. You are filled with envy and malice."

"Do you know what?" put in a young man who squinted very markedly. "Let us leave talking about the fair. We will be at it all day to-morrow. We will be dead tired of it long before the day is done. Let us talk about something altogether different."

And, the people at once began to talk about worldly affairs—about the prospect of citrons for the festivals that were coming soon—about the happenings of the last week at the House of Learning, and naturally about war.

Everyone was talking and smoking. The *samovar* was hissing and bubbling, and the room was filled with smoke and steam. And, on the oven the supper was cooking—the usual Saturday-night *Borst*, and goodness only knows what else beside.

"Where were you?" asked Dvossa-Malka of her daughter-in-law.

"Only out on the Monastery Road."

"How is it outside? I hope to God the weather will keep fine until the summer fairs are at an end. But, what is the matter with you, my daughter? Does your head ache that you are so pale? Rochalle, would you like to go and lie down on your bed?"

At these words the company turned round, and seeing Rochalle's white face they all cried, as with one accord, that she had been made dizzy by the fumes that came from the charcoal of the *samovar*. She went to her won room to lie down, leaving the people deep in a discussion on the dangers of charcoal fumes—the fumes which were in themselves so trifling—a mere nothing, one might say—a little smoke, and which yet had the strange power of injuring a person that he died of the effects. Someone told a story which had happened at a house of a friend of his grandfather's—peace be unto him! The whole family had almost been sent out of the world by the fumes of the charcoal.

Another told a more remarkable story—how the whole household belonging to an uncle of his had been very nearly poisoned through eating a certain fish, the name of which was "Marenka." They were all so ill that the doctors could hardly manage to drag them back from the jaws of death.

They talked so long until they came at last to the old, inevitable subject of death.

"No matter what one starts talking about, one is sure to talk of death before long," remarked someone.

"I must go and see what her ladyship is doing, said Moshe-Mendel, his voice breaking the silence which had suddenly fallen upon all present. He got up, and left the room.

"Help! To the rescue, friends!" The words came from the room into which Moshe-Mendel had gone. The people rushed forward; and, when they were come into the room, they found that Rochalle was lying across her bed, her limbs stuff, her eyes staring and glazed, and beside her stood Moshe-Mendel, half dead with fear.

"What is it? Who has fainted? Water! Quick! Water, water!" everyone shouted together; but, no one stirred from his place.

"Oh, to the devil with you all!" cried Dvossa-Malka, bringing a pitcher of water from another room. She splashed the face of Rochalle, who was pale as death.

"Let us call in the doctor," suggested Moshe-Mendel, in a voice that was quite unlike his own.

"The doctor, the doctor!" was repeated by each of the guests in turn, as they looked into each other's eyes.

"You ought to tie her hands with a handkerchief, and pinch her nose!"

"Her nose—her nose!" they all cried; but, no one stirred a hand or foot.

"That's right! Pinch it tighter, Dvossa-Malka, tighter!" The guests encouraged the mistress of the house in her work of rubbing Rochalle's temples, pinching her nose, and sprinkling her with cold water. She persevered for so long until Rochalle was at last restored to consciousness.

"She looked around her in a dazed, stupefied way, as if she did not at all know where she was, and she asked: "Where am I? I am very hot—hot!"

"Go out of the way, everybody!" said Dvossa-Malka, driving them out of the room like sheep. And, she and Moshe-Mendel found themselves alone with Rochalle, who all this time had never taken her eyes from Moshe-Mendel's face.

"What happened to you, daughter?" asked her mother-in-law.

"What ails you?" asked Moshe-Mendel, bending low over her, until his face was on a level with hers.

"Let your mother go out of the room," was Rochalle's whispered reply.

"Mother, excuse me, but would you be so kind as to leave us to ourselves?" said Moshe-Mendel. He went to the room door with his mother, and then returned to Rochalle's beside.

"Tell me, what ails you, Rochalle?" asked he, in a voice that was full of real concern and tenderness, for the very first time.

"Oh, Moshe-Mendel, you must swear to me that you

will tell no one, and that everything will remain a dead secret between us. Promise me you will forgive me for what I have done against you.... If it had not been for Chaya-Ettel—peace be unto her—if it had not been for her reminder.... Oh, if it had not been for Chaya-Ettel.... Oh, Moshe-Mendel, my dear one!"

"Bethink you, Rochalle, of what you are saying. You are overheated, and are talking at random. Who and what is Chaya-Ettel?"

"My school-friend, Chaya-Ettel, the orphan girl—peace be unto her!—she has gone, long ago, to the world of Eternal Truth. But, I have seen her in my dreams many times of late. But, now to-day.... Oh, Moshe-Mendel, bend down your head to me, lower and nearer. Ah, that's right.... I am afraid. ....I am filled with remorse.... Oh, I am filled with the bitterest remorse."

And, Rochalle nestled closer and closer to Moshe-Mendel until she was in his arms. The room was dark, only a single ray of light came in to them from the next room, through the door. Rochalle and Moshe-Mendel could barely make out one another's faces. But, their eyes were riveted on each other; and, gradually a fire was enkindled in the hearts of both—a fire such as exists on the heart of a man or woman once in a lifetime, when the heart speaks, and not the tongue, when the eyes are eloquent and not the mouth.

"Tell me, Moshe-Mendel, my true one, am I so very dear to you!"

"What a question!" answered Moshe-Mendel. "You are rooted deep in the very fibres of my being, like a— I can't say myself like what." And, he could find no words in which to express his love for Rochalle. But, his sincerity was evident to her. It was beyond a doubt. He was quite as sincere and perhaps more sincere than the fine fellow who had the gift of expressing himself with ease and eloquence on every occasion.

But, this much was certain, the husband and wife who had been married for more than a year already were only now discovering that they really loved one another to distraction. This was the first opportunity they had ever had of talking freely and openly with one another, and they had found out that they were the very complement of one another. They were cooing like two doves in the mating season.

When Rochalle felt a little eased, and had nothing more to say, Moshe-Mendel too was at a loss. He was still sitting with his arms about her, and he began to hum softly from the "Elijah" they had all been singing earlier in the evening. "Elijah the Prophet, Elijah the Tishbite... of Gilead."

And, Rochalle said to him, "I have something to ask of you, Moshe-Mendel. Tell me. Will you grant it me or not?"

"For instance? What is it you wish me to grant you? Speak Rochalle, and you will get it of me. Even if you ask me the fabulous golden plate of heaven, I will get it for you."

"It is enough! Moshe-Mendel, you have lived in your parents' house on their bounty quite long enough. You are not a school-boy now. We have a few *roubles*, thank God! Let us leave this, and go live in my village, in Yehupetz, amongst my people, my family and friends. When I am with you I will be as happy as the day is long. We will be by ourselves. We have had enough of being waited on hand and foot. I am dead sick of it. I hate it. I can't stand it any longer.... We are here with your parents, and we are like strangers to one another, black strangers!"

Moshe-Mendel sat quite still. He said nothing, but tried to think. He looked at Rochalle with some wonderment. He shook himself and began to sing the "Elijah" all over again.

"Oh, that's all right," he said after a few minutes. "Why not? Let it be even next week, if you like."

"I get you to do everything I want, Moshe-Mendel—everything!" said Rochalle, regarding him with a newly born feeling of admiration. "Oh, yes, we will live by ourselves henceforth. I will look after the household; and, I will tend to the very least of your wants as if you were the apple of my eye. Oh, Moshe-Mendel, you were always so distracted, so excited by outside matters, that I never heard a kind word from you. But, tonight you are so changed towards me—so changed...."

"Elijah the Prophet," sang Moshe-Mendel softly, as if to himself—"Elijah the Tishbite... of Gilead!"

And, there in the parlour, amongst the men, a different argument was being carried on. They had told each other all the jokes they knew; and, in due course, they came to the question of why Isaac-Naphtali's daughter-in-law had fainted away so suddenly. One said that she had had an Evil Eye cast upon her. A second contradicted that statement and put forward the contention that she had caught a chill through standing in a draughty passage. Whilst a third, a grizzled Jew, who had long ago married off the youngest of all his children, gave his opinion at length:

"Listen to me. I have three daughters-in-law, and I know what I am talking about. I tell you that it is nothing at all. Believe me, it will pass off. Young women often take like that for no reason, and there is nothing in the least to be alarmed at."

Dvossa-Malka beamed at him with satisfaction. "Well, well," she said, pretending to be anxious about Rochalle. "Go away with your talk. It is better to go and have a look at supper on the oven than to stand and listen to you. You must all be very hungry. The supper is later than usual tonight."

XXV A YEAR LATER

"A tame story!" the reader may possibly exclaim, feeling highly dissatisfied with the fare I have set before him, because of the fact that he has been brought up on the "highly interesting romances" in which there is hanging, and drowning, and poisoning, and shooting on every page. Or, in which perhaps a poor teacher becomes a duke, and a servant-girl a princess, and an under-gardener a troubadour. But, what can I do? Am I to blame if amongst our people there are neither dukes nor princesses? If amongst us there are only ordinary women and musicians, plain young women with no dreams of marvelous transformations, and working men who live from hand to mouth?

But, of what avail are my explanations? At this stage the reader may think what he likes. Once I have succeeded in bringing him so far as this he will not refuse to come a little further with me. He will surely have some curiosity to know what became of Rochalle, and what became of Stempenyu.

A whole year has passed! (What is a single year in a man's life?) And, once again we find ourselves in the house of Isaac-Naphtali, at the close of the Sabbath day; and, the very same persons are gathered together again that we found there on that memorable night, a twelve-month back, when Moshe-Mendel promised Rochalle that he would take her back to her own village, in Yehupetz. Nobody has changed by so much as a hair. As usual, they are talking of the fair, of the difficulties of making a living, of the doings of their children, and of the things which took place in the village recently. And, by and by they come to Moshe-Mendel and Rochalle, who are now living in Yehupetz.

"Show it here, Dvossa-Malka—the letter that the children sent us from Yehupetz," said Isaac-Naphtali to his wife. And, on getting it, he added, "Here, read it for yourself, Reb Youdel."

"Let him read it," said Reb Youdel, turning to the young man with the squint.

The young man with the squint took the letter, and read it with great ease and rapidity. It ran as follows:—

"Peace and all good to my father—the famous man of piety, the wonderful teacher and rabbi, Isaac-Naphtali, son of Reb Moshe-Joseph, of blessed memory! And, also to my beloved mother, whose piety and fame and virtue are like unto the piety and fame and virtue of Esther and Abigail of old—to my mother, whose name is beautiful— Dvossa, Malka, the daughter of Reb Moshe-Mendel, of blessed memory! And to this whole household I send greetings and peace.

"As the sun shines out through the dark clouds of the blue heavens there on high, in the highest heavens, from out of the blue windows..."

"No, no!" shouted a chorus of voices; not that. "It is only—only—poetry, boyish things, childish nonsense. Read further what is on the other side."

The young man with the squint turned over the page, and read:

"And as regards your question concerning my livelihood, and business that is carried on here in Yehupetz—I must tell you first of all..."

"Ah, that's what we want to hear!" said the people, satisfied at last. "Read, young man, read further!"

"I must tell you, first of all, that drapery is sold here in smallwares; but smallwares not so much as drapery. Embroideries are not bad either—not worse than with you. Woolens are dear here, like gold itself. Sugar and flour and bran are also good to trade in. They are sent across the frontier, and Jews earn a fine lot of money through them. Yehupetz is a blessed land! The town itself is terrible. It is worth a man's while to look at it. In short, it is a different world here in Yehupetz. You may come upon such Jews whom you would never dream of calling Jews. And there is a good trade done in paper here, too. There is trading in everything. And Jews turn around on the Exchange, and buy and sell all sorts of bonds. Brokers make lots of money.

"My wife sends you her friendliest greetings. She is also writing to you herself. May God preserve you all. And I hope we will hear from you the best of news. Amen!

"*P.S.*—Then I must tell you that a shop like mine is in the very front of the Alexandrevitz Street. And the income is not all bad. Blessed be He!"

"My wife Rochalle—may she live long!—has learned the business already and can talk to a customer. But as to buying at the fairs—I do that myself. I have credit amongst merchants in Moscow and Lodz. With Moscow it is not bad to deal. Moscow sells honestly and likes a Jewish customer. If a man is doing badly, Moscow comes to his aid and does not let him go down altogether.

"Dwelling-houses are very dear here. For two rooms and a kitchen I pay 175 *roubles* a year, and have to get my own wood and water. Everything thing is dear here—like gold. Mostly the Jews are middlemen; and of Jewish middlemen there are many here. And Jews earn an honest *rouble* through it. In short, Yehupetz is a place of business. May God give us health and strength, and I hope to hear the same from you.

"From me, your son, who is anxious for your happiness every day—Moshe-Mendel—the son of my beloved father, Isaac-Naphtali of Tasapevka.

"Greetings to my dear uncle and dear aunt, and his whole family.

"Greetings to the wealthy one, Reb Youdel, and his whole family.

"Greetings to the wealthy one, Reb Dauber, and his whole family.

"Greetings to the wealthy one, Madame Stessa-Beila, and her whole family.

My son Joseph—may his light continue to shine!—sends you all his friendliest greetings.

THE ABOVE NAMED!"

* * *

"I greet my highly honoured and deeply-appreciated father-in-law—may you live long! I wish to let you know that I am in good health, thank God! May the Lord send me no worse. Also, my little Joseph sends you his greetings; and he thanks my mother-in-law for the little shirt, many times over. If God lets him live and is willing to have it so, Joseph will go to school in three or four years' time. He will learn diligently, please God! And please God! he will grow up a pious Jew. May the Lord send him long years! Amen! Dear Mother-in-law, if you can make for my little Joseph a little cap and a pair of little shoes from embroidery I would thank you very much. I am so much occupied with business and I do not wish to take a nurse for little Joseph. It is not worth while. I hired a little girl and pay her four *roubles* a month. She rocks the cradle and drives the cow to the meadow. You ought to see what a cow I bought. She gives four quarts of milk a day—beautiful milk; and I have plenty of butter and cheese. But Moshe-Mendel has taken a sudden dislike towards all these things. Please give him a scolding, I beg of you. Joseph has just wakened up. He is hungry, poor dear child!

"I close my letter and send regards to all our relatives and friends. I beg of you to reply to me, and I remain

your most affectionate and faithful daughter-in-law,
ROCHALLE"

"Nu!" cried Berrel the Fat One—I hope that my children never be worse off than Moshe-Mendel and Rochalle.

"You are sinning, Dvossa-Malka; you are sinning," said Youdel. "Yes, you are sinning."

"You are right, Reb Youdel. Thanks be to the Blessed Name! They are indeed well off. May no Evil Eye fall upon them! But I am full of pain. I can never forget them."

And, Dvossa-Malka set out to explain to Reb Youdel all the noble qualities of her daughter-in-law, down to the minutest detail. And, she wept copiously because she could never forget her. Around her in the room the people were talking about Yehupetz, and the merchants of Yehupetz. Afterwards they got out glasses, and drank a toast, holding the glasses in their hands for a long time. They wished each other everything that was good. Nor did they forget to add that they hoped fervently to see all the Children of Israel flourishing and joyous.

The supper was placed on table, the dishes sending out a fragrance through the whole room.

The company grew flushed, and talkative, and joyous. They talked, and they talked, and forgot all about Moshe-Mendel and Rochalle and the town of Yeheputz, and everything connected with it.

But there is one person who cannot forget Rochalle. Perhaps the reader has guessed that Stempenyu is here referred to. Yes, Stempenyu is the person referred to. But, who is there can describe the pain that was his? Who can read his heart and measure his agony?

"How I suffer! How my heart aches!" he says to himself again and again. "And, she never confessed anything. She never wrote down two broken words to tell me that she was going away. Phew! It was shameful!"

Nothing of the sort had ever happened to Stempenyu before, though there had happened to him all sorts of strange things. And, often nasty things, with bad endings. But, such an aggravating thing, such a downfall as that which was connected with the flight of Rochalle he never dreamt would happen to him. Stempenyu, who had been so intimately connected with all the nobility and gentry, whose daughters had shown him their open admiration—Stempenyu, about whom the beautiful noblewoman had gone mad, and for despair of winning him had committed suicide—Stempenyu, who had talked in French and German with the greatest ladies in the land—it was terrible that this same Stempenyu should have come to suffer so much and so keenly through an ordinary, commonplace young woman!

"It makes my heart ache to think of her," Stempenyu confessed to his company of musicians. "That young woman makes my heart ache every time I think of her. And, I should like to go after her to Yehupetz, if it were not for—if it were not that—" Stempenyu was confused. He looked around him at each of the men in turn. And, they knew well whom it was that he was searching for with his eyes. They were all very fond of Stempenyu, and passionately devoted to him. They were ready to go through fire and water for him. And, as much as they loved Stempenyu, they hated Freidel. They could not bear to look at her because of her miserliness, and her love of money, and all her mean, despicable ways.

"Oh, yes; when he was a bachelor," the musicians would say—"when he was a young man, a *rouble* was nothing at all to him; and, one could get round him easily. One could get a loan of a three-*rouble* note from him never to be repaid. And, even a five-*rouble* note. Sometimes one got a present from him in the ordinary way. But, now, since that wicked woman has him in her talons, he himself might die for a *kopek*-piece. He might be hung for a *groschen*. The old times are gone for ever, and the glorious suppers Stempenyu used to make for us and the jolly knocking about from place to place.

Nowadays, one might as well lie down in a ditch and die, because one gets withered and swollen up with hunger. The whole year one has to go without bread; and, when the season for weddings comes round at last, she never even offers a man, out of mere decency itself, so much as a bite of bread or a glass of tea. She never has the good manners to offer a man a meal—may the worms devour her from head to toe!"

"Believe me, there are times nowadays when a man is actually hungry. And, it is terrible to suffer for want of food. But, if she were to place a heap of gold before me, I would not demean myself by tasting so much as a single crumb of hers—the vixen!"

"How does he manage to live with her—with such a female Turk—with such a hag—a she-devil? I would have poisoned her, or hung her up long ago, as sure as you see me alive!"

"Oh, Stempenyu! You have been buried alive! You are lying in the earth and baling cakes, as the saying has it!"

That was how the musicians spoke of Stempenyu. They saw how he suffered, and they felt keenly what he was feeling, out of sympathy, though he had not said more than a word or two of what was really taking place within him to anybody. When he suffered most he was dumb, not knowing what to say.

Whenever Freidel when to market, or when she was occupied in taking pledges, or in attending to her customers, it was not so bad. Stempenyu could treat the musicians to cigarettes. They would sit and chat, and tell one another stories of bygone times. They smoked and talked as if the whole world was theirs. But, the very moment Freidel crossed the threshold their hearts were chilled and they crept from the room one by one.

"Just see how they have filled the room with smoke, as if this were a public house," she said, sniffling here and there, and looking daggers at the remains of the cigarettes in the packet, "They only want to smoke—to puff, and nothing else. My head aches from your cigarettes. You will make me ill. You imagine, Stempenyu, that it is good to smoke? Be advised by me, Stempenyu. Give up smoking. My soul, believe me, it is injurious to your health."

"What do you care, Freidel, about my health! Sat that you begrudge me the money I spend on tobacco, and have done with it. What is the use of pretending?"

"What do you say to him? He talks of pretenses! I mean only his good, and he talks only of pretenses. There's for you! I suppose I do begrudge you everything because of the beautiful day I have had, fighting, and sweating, and eating out my heart with aggravation, and without taking in a *kopek*. And, along with this I was abused as if I were a servant girl—worse than any servant girl. They called me names, and blackened my character, until it was as mud that lies in the middle of the road... And, the goods are not sold. They are lying there and rotting."

"I should like to know, Freidel, devil, why you protest so much. Why do you stint and scrape? Have your children fallen upon you, demanding from you the Lord knows what?"

"Just look at him, I beg of you, the innocent! He knows nothing. One has to put everything on the tip of his tongue. I suppose I carry everything off to my mother—eh, Stempenyu? Or perhaps I eat everything up myself? A glutton and a drunkard like your wife is a terrible person to come upon without warning, eh, Stempenyu? Look into my eyes, Stempenyu. Can you do that?"

"Did I say you eat up everything? On the contrary..."

"You say—you say—I know what you say. Perhaps you ought to male complaints, Stempenyu? You ought to rebel against the Lord because He sent you such a thriftless wife—such a wife as I am, who can make two *groschens* out of one at any time, and who keeps your interest in mind day and night. Yes, tell me what you are short of, and how much you are losing. You are silent. I should only like to know this much. What would you have had to lean on with your fiddle this day if you had not had me for your wife?"

"Oh! Ha!"

"You would surely have been in 'Oh! Ha!' It seems that you have forgotten what condition you were in when you married me. You hadn't a shirt on your back. You hadn't a pair of socks that were not full of holes. You had not a pillow to rest your head on, nor a pillow-case either. And, you were earning lots of money. Where did it all go to?"

"I'm running to give you an account of my earnings before I married you!"

"Ah, that's what's the matter with you, Stempenyu. You cannot bear to be told the exact truth. And, you have grievances against those who beat their heads against the wall for you—who toil, and sweat, and crawl on all fours, so to speak, and who deny themselves a crust of bread, and lead a life of continuous hardship for your sake. For him? Perhaps you can tell me what good deeds he has done to deserve all this? He will probably but a golden tombstone over my head.... Woe is me!"

"What have I done to you? Who is touching you?"

"What more can you do to me? You have done enough. You have darkened my life for me. You came upon a young girl, a child, and with a false look of your eyes you betrayed her. You promised me everything— golden mountains. You made yourself out a liar from head to foot. How well off I should have been if I had never known you. I should have sought out someone who would have understood me, and cared for me. But, I would not have been Stempenyu's wife! What a piece of good fortune I have come upon!"

"Well, perhaps you are sorry that you married me? Well, there is a rabbi in Tasapevka, and a river. And, one can write out a divorce."

"Ah, ah, ah! So that is what you are driving at! You squeezed it out at last. You think that I do not know you were looking in that direction? You want to rid yourself of me? I know Stempenyu, I know. You cannot fool me. Am I standing in your light, Stempenyu? But, have I deserved this of you? I ask you to tell me, as a favour, how I have deserved this from you. Let me also know my offence."

"This!" replied Stempenyu, waving his hand mystically. He went into his room, locked the door, and took down his fiddle from the wall. The fiddle was now his only consolation, his only friend in the wide world. The fiddle was the only medium through which he could attain to forgetfulness of his bitter disappointment. It brought back to his mind the days of his childhood, and youth, and early manhood. It reminded him, too, of the liberty he had lost for ever and ever. Many different persons came up before him, like ghosts, as he played. With the music that he drew from his fiddle he was charmed into vain imaginings. Many pictures of the might-have-been stood before him as he played, and dozens of pictures of the days that were gone past recalling. He was like a man standing before an enormous panorama. Each picture came up in its turn, stayed a moment—and was gone, to give place to another picture equally pleasurable, and equally painful.

But, there was one picture which invariably stood out more strongly than any of the others—one which he could never hope to forget, much as he might have wished it. That one picture was of Rochalle, with her shining face and blue eyes and long lashes and snow-white neck, and the sweet, gentle smile for which he was ready to lay down everything—everything.

Stempenyu went on playing and playing. He played for a long, long time, so that Rochalle's image might remain beside him, conjured up by the music. He wished that it would stay with him and not vanish, as all the other pictures vanished in their turn. He was so full of yearning towards her that it was some comfort to him if she was with him even in imagination. The very memory of her was dear to him—very dear.

At that period, Stempenyu played as he never played before, and as he never played again. He reached the zenith of his power in those unhappy weeks and months immediately following the departure of Rochalle from the village, and the consequent shattering of all his bright hopes. For, he had been more deeply touched by Rochalle than by anyone he had ever come across in all his life. And, therefore, it would be safe to say that whoever did no hear him at this period can have no real idea of what his playing was like.

And, that's how it is always. We are filled with delight at the wondrous sweetness of the song which the little bird sings from its cage. The little bird is dreaming of green leaves, fresh flowers soaked with dew, balmy air, a burning sun, and a free world—a world without bars—a broad expanse of blue about which it may fly as it wishes. And, as it dreams, the little bird is overcome with the desire to sing—to pour out all the bitterness that is in its heart. And, so its singing is only another name for weeping, for expressing all the melting sorrows of its heart. And, we who listen to it are filled with delight because of the sweetness of the melody. We are filled with sheer joy at the passionate tenderness of the little bird's notes. And, we imagine that they have come forth through feelings of pleasure in the bird's heart such as are in our hearts. But, it is not so.

"She makes my heart ache with longing," said Stempenyu to his musicians for the hundredth time. "I long for her with my whole heart as if she were my own. I would go after her to Yehupetz, but for—"

And, Stempenyu looked about him on all sides. His eyes alighted on Freidel. She was muttering to herself as she bent over a box or corals, and silk scarves and a variety of embroideries.

Freidel had brought together a whole store of goods in her own house, and regarded herself as a merchant, after the fashion of the other merchants of the village.

Her mother, Ziporah the Fat One, often came to visit her. She was always telling Freidel that her father, Isaiah, longs for his daughter; and, that he sent her, Ziporah, to find out how she is. But, Freidel knows that this is a lie. She knows perfectly well that at home her mother is often short of bread to eat, and that she comes to her to break her fast, in spite of her pretenses to the contrary.

"Do you know what, my daughter?" she says. "You ought to make the butter cakes that I used to make long ago. They are delicious with chicory, and very nourishing. And, if one can digest them when made with a lot of butter, they are altogether delicious. And, for breakfast, there is nothing like hot goose-fat, just melted, with onions. Your father, if you remember, was always fond of that. It is very nourishing. Shall I go and get the fat out of the dish?"

And, by degrees, Ziporah gave herself up altogether to the task of inventing new dishes for every meal of the day—for breakfast, dinner, tea and supper. But, it cannot be said that Freidel was overpleased with this. The first few times, she made no comment, and seemed to be taking no notice. But, after about a week or so, she began to give hints to her mother. And, her mother paid her back in the same coin, until they came to quarreling openly, letting out on each other all their anger. Nor did they spare Stempenyu when he tried to make peace between them.

"It is not your business at all!" said Freidel to him. "Have no fear. I will not give my mother your property—the family heirlooms. Be quiet, Stempenyu."

"It's a lovely paradise!" cried the mother from her side of the room, with pronounced sarcasm. "An ox has a long tongue; but, it can't blow a horn. Amongst respectable folks a mother-in-law is treated with as much respect as a mother. I imagine I hear him reply: 'But, what respect do you get from your daughter?' What do they say? Cut of your notes to spite your face. And, he never even wags his tongue to reprove her. Do you call that a man? It is exactly as some people say, 'So long as one dances on the green, all is well.' I don't understand it at all. How is it he does not grow weary of all this? What my daughter is so proud of is more than I can tell. If one is lucky, even one's ox goes to calf. We have already seen such heroes as you are. Your father-in-law, Isaiah, was just as good a fiddler as you are. But—nothing! How do they say, 'A new broom sweeps clean.' In everything one must have good luck; and, if God will it, even a broom can shoot. But, Stempenyu, you ought to be offended with me because I am telling you the exact truth. And, though every dog is a master on his own doorstep, you must remember that I am no stranger to you. After all, I am your mother-in-law; and, when one plays with the cat, one must take her scratches for love-tokens."

Ziporah went on pouring out the words as from a full sack, as was usual with her when she was once started talking. But, Stempenyu would not hear her out. He left the room, and betook himself to his fiddle, as was his habit when his heart was heavy, and when his soul was full to overflowing with anger and resentment and regrets. He forgot, soon after he had started playing, all about his wife, and his mother-in-law, and his load of miseries.

And, once again there stood before him the image of

Rochalle....

"She fills my heart's heart with aching," he murmured, while his mind was busy trying to devise some means of seeing her in the flesh once more. "How and where is it possible to see her, even if only for a single instant?"

But, these are all empty dreams—vanity, and weariness of the flesh.

Stempenyu does not know that his little song is nearly sung, and that his little world has almost come to an end. He does not know that his black locks are getting thinner day by day, and that his burning eyes are slowly but surely losing their fiery glances, and that his white brow is falling into wrinkles. He has ceased to take the least interest in what befalls him. He is so deeply absorbed in his visions that he has neither eyes nor ears nor senses. He is stupid, and blind, and deaf before his time.

Foolish giant! Do not forget yourself. At your side stands your Delilah—the Delilah that lured you into her arms, and took you on her knee, and rocked you to sleep. And, while you slept, she cut off your locks of hair in which lay the source and origin of your great strength— all your abilities that lifted you up above other men. Your Delilah did unto you just as the Delilah of old did unto her husband, Samson the Strong, after which he was lost and ruined, and fell into the hands of the Philistines....

You have only one consolation left you in the world— only one—your little fiddle. Then play, Stempenyu— play on your fiddle, and we will listen....